BACK TO YOU

Steve Bates

2021 White Bird Publications, LLC

Copyright © 2021 by Steve Bates
Cover by E. Kusch

Published in the United States
by White Bird Publications, LLC, Texas
www.whitebirdpublications.com

ISBN 978-1-63363-495-4
eBook ISBN 978-1-63363-496-1
Library of Congress Control Number: 2020950314

PRINTED IN THE UNITED STATES OF AMERICA

For Jean and Jeffrey

Praise for "Back to You"

Most wondrous st'ry hast ev'r been writ.
    —W. Shakespeare

Why didn't I think of this?
    —A. Einstein

Knocked it right outta the park.
    —B. Ruth

Advances the cause of world peace.
    —M. Teresa

BACK TO YOU

**White Bird
Publications**

A BIG CITY; PRESENT DAY

Eddie Corbin scrutinized a massive dashboard crammed with unfamiliar dials and buttons and levers. Hoping to sound a horn, he began turning and pushing and sliding instruments. A low whine permeated the vehicle. Dashboard lights kicked off a spirited dance sequence. The hairs on his neck and arms stood on end.

Beyond the windshield, frantic shouts and trumpet blasts pierced the air. Eddie gaped as dozens of men clad in chain-mail armor fought with swords and axes in front of a moss-stained stone castle. Attackers placed wooden planks across a moat, but they were dispatched by what appeared to be boiling oil. Every time a combatant bit the dust, two more entered the fray.

"Man," observed Eddie, "this neighborhood has really gone to hell."

A female voice—friendly, yet firm—declared: "I do not recommend exiting the vehicle."

Eddie turned his head. "I'm sorry. I thought the food truck was empty. I was just trying to honk for the owner, man. I mean, woman."

"I am neither man nor woman. I am what you call an AI, an artificial intelligence. It is my duty to warn you about the hostilities surrounding this vehicle."

"Thanks. It does look pretty intense out there." Eddie hesitated, realizing that he was speaking to someone or something he couldn't see. "Do you have a name?"

"I am unit TT7970-44BES. Some people call me Bess."

"Nice to meet you, Bess. You don't happen to have any chocolate, do you?"

"I do not dispense food. My sole function is temporal transport."

"Bummer. So, what's all this D&D stuff?"

"This is the French region known as Normandy. The year is 1203."

"But why are people staging a medieval battle reenactment in an alley?"

"Allow me to clarify. As a result of your manipulation of the controls, we have traveled in space and time to witness a significant battle in European history. Would you prefer to visit a different location and time?"

Eddie recoiled as an ax-wielding fighter was shoved against his window and impaled with a sword. "Uh, yeah, that would be good."

Chris—he just went by Chris—was six-foot-five and a chiseled 225 pounds, with one of those symmetrical faces that are easy to forget. Wearing ragged jeans, a Pokemon T-shirt, and a Yankees cap, he drew scant attention from passersby as he traversed the same block of 16th Street twice in each direction. He crossed the street and repeated the process, but he still could not find the deli that he was certain existed there. The deli that made the most scrumptious pastrami on rye on the planet, perhaps the best pastrami on rye ever to delight human taste buds.

Reluctantly, Chris abandoned his quest, turned into an alley, and gazed dumbfounded at the empty space where just minutes earlier he had left his vehicle—one that would be so very dangerous in the wrong hands. He jogged up and down the narrow thoroughfare in a panic, searching for any clue to the fate of his transport. Then he leaned back against a concrete wall and slumped lifelessly to the pavement, disturbing a couple of rats trying to enjoy a peaceful lunch.

As much to the universe as to himself, he muttered: "What have I done?"

Tony Shaw possessed a scowl that could sink a thousand ships. He was practicing what he considered to be an exceptionally fierce facial contortion this morning. He directed it toward Eddie, staring intensely at him a few seconds for full effect, eyes bulging menacingly, before saying slowly: "That is absolutely the lamest excuse for being late for work I have ever heard."

The scowl was wasted on Eddie.

With his head shaved almost to the bone on both sides and a tall shock of curly brown hair up top, Eddie looked younger than his forty-two years. Holding down a maintenance job at a failing cable television network, sharing an apartment with his mom, and consuming junk food voraciously, his was a simple existence. Eddie didn't know the meaning of vexation. In fact, he didn't know the meaning of a lot of words. Once, he showed up for a salsa lesson with tomatoes, peppers and a bag of chips. He wouldn't apply for a job at a satellite radio company because he thought that he would have to work in orbit, and he was afraid of heights. Though shortchanged in intellect and sophistication, Eddie was generously endowed with the gift of geniality.

Not to mention curiosity. On this fateful day, he had been intrigued by the faded, barely legible words on the side of a food truck parked in an alley near his building: "Easter Island Cuisine". Eddie did not recall encountering this food truck before, and he knew just about every food truck in town. He had never heard of Easter Island, but the name conjured a land where gleeful youngsters stuffed themselves with chocolate bunnies and scampered across verdant lawns searching for colorful eggs.

The disappointment at finding no sweet treats in the food truck did not diminish Eddie's excitement about his discovery. Besides, Tony was just about the only person around who would listen to him.

"The time machine is parked right behind the building," said Eddie. "Let me prove it to you."

Tony was a British transplant, nearly sixty, nearly bald, nearly fat, and nearly ready to welcome his third ulcer. He was not a patient man. Nor was he a polite man. In fact, Tony had few redeeming personal or professional qualities. He was ideally suited to be the news director of the Hysteria Channel, which filled its airtime with nonstop arguing by talking heads and with other forms of acrimony. Unfortunately for Tony, he shouldered the daunting task of reversing the network's plummeting ratings. As it happened, on this day he also was late, for a budget meeting with insufferable executives. Eddie's absurd story gave Tony the excuse he craved to blow it off.

Tony mumbled something rude as Eddie escorted him out the back door, through the parking lot and to a rusted green Ford Pinto with substantial body damage.

Tony sniffed Eddie's breath. "Are you drunk? Or stoned?"

"I disguised the time machine as a 1974 Pinto because that's the model with the exploding gas tank. No one will come near it."

Tony rolled his eyes.

"Just watch," said Eddie. "Bess, I'd like you to meet Tony. He would like to take a ride."

Two doors opened. "Nice trick," said Tony. The men

settled into the front seats.

"Hello, Tony," said Bess. "Where and when would you like to go?"

He decided to play along. "Might as well go someplace special. How about a rendezvous with the Three Wise Men?"

"You mean Moe, Larry, and Curly?" asked Eddie. "I'd prefer to visit the very first McDonald's."

After some discussion, the men settled on witnessing the sinking of the Titanic. In almost no time, their vehicle was rocking above Atlantic Ocean waves less than 100 yards from the doomed ship. Lifeboats were being lowered. Anxious voices wafted across the water.

Tony rolled down a window. The salt spray chilled his face. "Whoa. This can't be a video playback. That really is the Titanic."

Eddie's expression reflected the passengers' pain. "Can we rescue some of them?"

"I do not advise it," Bess stated. "If you were to exit the vehicle and interact with the environment or people, you could generate serious conundrums."

"Are those the drums that guy in AC/DC plays?" inquired Eddie.

"Let me try it this way: Have you heard of the butterfly effect?"

"Yeah. Those critters chewed black holes in my best sweater," responded Eddie. "Actually, my only sweater."

"I think that what Bess is trying to say," said Tony, "is that the things you do during time travel could have unintended consequences."

"Thank you," said Bess. "By the way, can you tell me what happened to Chris?"

"Who's Chris?" asked Eddie.

"But we don't have to worry," said Tony, "as long as we don't do something stupid like shoot our moms before they could give birth to us. What Bess is saying is like the 'do not attempt' warning at the bottom of the screen in the commercial where a guy jumps out of a plane, bounces off a series of hot air balloons, slides through a sunroof, and lands gently in the seat of a six-figure sports car next to a fashion model holding his martini. It's just rubbish the lawyers make up to justify their jobs."

Tony's scowl morphed into something approaching a smile. "You know, a time machine might be exactly what we need to save our sorry excuse for a cable network."

Bess sighed.

Reporters Deidre Lucchesi and Wade Braun sat sullenly at opposite ends of a wooden table bearing the scars of decades of cigarette mishaps and pounded fists. The cramped conference room was also home to weeks-old pizza boxes, shoulder-high stacks of paper, and VCR tapes coated in a decade's worth of dust. A TV showed two Hysteria Channel forecasters screaming at each other in front of a weather map. One forecaster insisted that it would be sunny and dry on Tuesday; the other contended that there would be intermittent showers. The men exchanged insults and fenced with their pointer sticks. After the sticks broke, they wrestled and threw punches. One pulled a gun.

"It's so lame that they are only allowed rubber bullets," commented Wade. "No wonder no one watches us."

Deidre did not deign to respond. Tall and thin, with dark brown eyes and nearly straight, shoulder-length brown hair, Deidre was the antithesis of the assertive, bleach-blonde women who dominated cable shows. She never really smiled, though now and again the corners of her mouth curled up slightly with a hint of pleasure, particularly when she surprised an interview subject with a particularly probing question. Her demeanor concealed a seething core of competitiveness, however. She was the kind of person who even studied for an eye exam. Deidre had arrived at the network less than a year earlier, after completing graduate school with high honors. She had no friends in the building and seemed to have no interest in making any.

The few insomniacs and just plain angry people who tuned in to the Hysteria Channel regularly had become all too familiar with Wade's square jaw and well-practiced if insincere smile. A one-time high school star athlete, Wade dropped out of college after two years, but his blue eyes, flashy wardrobe, journalistic instincts, and amazing luck had taken him far in a short time in his chosen line of work. He was particularly proud of his perfect mane of jet-black hair, which he had insured for $1-million. If there were such a thing as a narcissist's narcissist, Wade would be that guy.

Tony burst into the room. "Eddie found a real time machine. You two will be using it in a series of groundbreaking live assignments," he blurted out, almost hyperventilating. "The program will be called 'Yore Right'. That's y-o-r-e, as in days of yore, not y-o-u-r."

"You mean, not y-o-u-apostrophe-r-e," said Deidre.

"Whatever," said Tony. "We can't bloody well call it '60 Minutes', now can we? Anyway, I did some intense research before settling on the subject of our first episode."

"You? Intense research?" scoffed Wade.

"Okay, I went on Wikipedia. But it will be fabulous," claimed Tony.

Wade shook his head, certain that his boss was completely and irreversibly out of his mind.

"I'm curious," said Deidre. "Where did this alleged time machine come from?"

"I don't know or care," responded Tony. "Maybe some future Hysteria Channel executive sent it back in time to us in order to save the network."

"But if there were such a future executive to send it back, we had already been saved and the action was not necessary," pointed out Deidre.

"Don't go beating those conundrums," Tony said. "Here's how the show will work: Eddie will be your navigator and tech support guy, but he has strict instructions not to leave the time machine during an episode. He's going to place tiny, almost invisible cameras and microphones on your clothes. Bess—she's the queen of the machine—says she will make your clothes and hair appear appropriate for whatever time and place you go. Only your face will look the same. Speech will get translated both ways. The machine can be disguised to blend into the background wherever you are."

His face began to take on a blue tint, so he paused to breathe.

"Here's the catch: You can't go more than 300 yards from the time machine, or your appearance and speech will revert to normal. That would expose you as being from the 21st century and would ruin the authenticity of the program."

"You're serious about this," said Wade.

"Deadly. We're promoting the living daylights out of this show. You're on in one hour."

A BIG CITY/UKRAINE

Using the Pinto's rear-view mirror, Wade inspected his teeth to make sure nothing was stuck between them. Then he smoothed his hair.

"Perhaps you forgot, your precious hair won't be visible in 3,500 B.C.," observed Deidre.

"You're just jealous," hissed Wade. 'You know why you'll never make it big in this business? You're not a blonde, and you have an IQ of 150. Nobody wants to watch brunettes with big brains and small—"

"Thirty seconds to showtime," interjected Eddie.

Bess said tersely: "Ask for Ivan."

The reporters' eyes widened as the view of the sunny company parking lot was supplanted by dense fog. Rain splattered lightly on the windows.

Wade took a deep breath, exhaled, and smiled. "This is Wade Braun reporting from thousands of years back in time. We're taking you to witness the invention of the wheel in a region that, in our time, is part of Ukraine."

He and Deidre exited the vehicle into a misty, muddy clearing edged by a semicircle of thatched huts. They approached a man dressed in layers of light brown animal skins and dark boots who was using primitive hand tools to chisel a boulder that was about five feet wide. Wade couldn't take his eyes off of Deidre, who looked stunning in the form-hugging, knee-length hides that Bess projected in place of her actual clothes.

"Excuse me, are you Ivan?" Deidre asked the worker.

"Yes."

"Are you making a wheel?"

"Yes."

"Did you invent it?"

"No. That was the other Ivan." He continued his work.

Peering through the fog, the reporters could discern a second man chiseling a large boulder about thrity yards away. "Prepare to witness history," announced Wade as they slogged toward the worker.

"Are you Ivan?" Deidre asked. "The Ivan who invented the wheel?"

"I am Ivan," the man stated. "But you want the Ivan beyond those huts."

The reporters could almost hear Tony cursing across the millennia as their body cameras revealed nothing but fog for a couple of minutes. Finally, Deidre and Wade came upon several men who were putting finishing touches on a large wooden platform with two axles and four stone wheels. An elephant watched nervously from a cage.

"How thrilling," commented Wade. "Remember, you saw this seminal event on the Hysteria Channel."

Deidre addressed the workers. "Excuse me, which one of you is Ivan?"

Several men raised hands.

"Mind if we watch?"

They shrugged. Then they opened the cage, used poles to nudge the elephant out of the cage and onto the platform, tied it in place, and began to pull the vehicle themselves with thick ropes.

"Hey guys, just a thought," said Wade. "Had you considered using the elephant to—ouch!"

After Deidre kicked him, she whispered: "We can't get involved."

To the home audience, she observed: "These intrepid inventors have some kinks to work out. But you have just witnessed a significant event in human history. Back to you in the studio."

Wade didn't seem to remember or care that they were still broadcasting live. "Deidre, I don't think 'back to you' is appropriate. Shouldn't it be 'forward to you', given that we are in the past?"

She refused to take the bait. "What an incredible moment in history."

The men stopped pulling the vehicle. One pointed at the newcomers and shouted: "They are talking to invisible spirits. They must be witches."

Said another: "Run them over!"

The men strained their considerable muscles and turned the vehicle in the direction of Deidre and Wade, who fell repeatedly while trying to run on the slick field. The locals were incredibly strong and started to gain on the journalists.

Panting, Deidre and Wade stumbled back into the clearing. Said Wade: "Tell me again how the time machine is disguised."

"Eddie said it would look like a thatched hut."

They faced several nearly identical thatched huts shrouded by fog.

Wade started to run. "I'm getting out of here!"

"Don't! You'll lose your disguise if you go more than 300 yards from the machine."

Wade settled on pacing frantically, calling out "Eddie!" repeatedly. The natives emerged from the fog and bore down on the reporters.

Deidre noticed a smell that seemed out of place. At first,

she could not identify it. Then, it came to her: a corn dog. The odor emanated from the hut on the far left. She reached through the hut's entryway, found the time machine's open door, shoved Wade inside, and followed him. Deidre slammed the door and shouted: "Home!"

A BIG CITY; PRESENT DAY

Like so many people who found themselves near the Hysteria Channel building—or any other storefront, restaurant, bar, PC, laptop, tablet, or cellphone that displayed a TV image— Chris watched in fascination as the first episode of "Yore Right" unfolded. He committed himself then and there to putting a stop to this perilous program. He would absolutely, totally nip it in the bud.

As soon as he could figure out how.

"You're now officially a time machine pilot and location scout," said Tony, leaning back in his fake leather chair.

"Does that mean I get a raise?" said Eddie. He was pretty sure that he knew the answer.

"Hell, no. You should be grateful that you're getting to see things almost no other person has ever dreamed of seeing--instead of changing lightbulbs."

Eddie could see his point.

"I'll do you a favor," said Tony, in that tone that even Eddie knew meant that no real favor was forthcoming. "I won't make you use your vacation days during time travel."

"I haven't taken a vacation since I started work here, except for that Star Trek convention back in 2002." Realizing that the conversation was over, Eddie exited, dropping by the cafeteria for some snacks on his way to the time machine. He explained his mission to Bess.

"Are you sure you want to do this?" she inquired. Though she was an AI and was supposed to respond to the demands of humans, she and other AIs were programmed to help people avoid doing things to themselves—and to other people—that might cause them harm. She knew that helping Eddie visit future times and places that could serve as destinations for episodes of "Yore Right" was fraught with danger.

"Remember that discussion we had about conund— I mean, about things turning out badly during travel to the past?" she said. "Multiply that danger by ten to the fifth power for travel to the future."

"I wasn't so good at math. Is that bad?"

"It's real bad."

"Okay. I won't get out of the machine. I promise."

DEEP SPACE; DATE UNKNOWN

Something evil this way came.

Picture a drop of water condensing on the bottom of a smooth rock and tumbling into a bottomless underground cistern, creating unseen and unheard impact waves. In this manner began the ripple in the space-time fabric that accompanied the arrival of the demon. The disruption commenced in no particular time or place—and in every time and place. Its effects were so subtle that no human or manmade device could detect it.

The RRRRBAI sensed it. The RRRRBAI was not happy.

A BIG CITY/MESOPOTAMIA

The reporters took their seats in the time machine and braced themselves for episode two.

"Sorry about the confusion regarding Ivan," Bess told them. "The farther we go into the past, the less accurate my database is."

"No problem," said Wade, summoning as much bravado as he could manage. "We humans are quite resourceful."

Eddie checked the supply of beef jerky in his shirt pocket. "Thirty seconds until we go live," he announced. "Next stop, Mesopotamia, one million B.C."

Bess transported them to a rolling, picturesque landscape with tall trees, winding streams, and clusters of dark green bushes. Deidre and Wade exited the time machine near the base of a sun-drenched hill. The reporters, who appeared to be dressed in tan hides, trudged up to a cave opening and shouted "hello!"

A shaggy human figure appeared. "Who's there?" said the shaggy person, apparently male, dressed in skins similar to those Bess was displaying for the reporters.

"Just two people who were in the neighborhood and were hoping to meet the guy who invented fire," said Wade. "It sounds useful."

The cave dweller smiled. "That it is. Come in."

The cave was dark and dank and smelled like a frat house on a Sunday morning.

"But please wipe your feet by the entrance," said the cave dweller. "The missus is a stickler about not tracking dirt into the house."

Wade took the lead. "Did you indeed invent fire?"

"Ha," said a second shaggy human figure, who approached the visitors from a dim recess of the cave. "Did Thran try to sell you that story that he invented fire?"

Thran looked down at his extremely large feet.

"He's been bragging all over the hillsides. 'Look at me, I invented fire! Look at me!' Ha."

The hearts of two 21st century humans sank.

"Alright," said Thran. "Maybe I did not *invent* fire, because it can be caused by natural phenomena such as lightning. But I learned how to manage it, and I told others about it. There, are you happy?"

The apparently female shaggy person grunted, indicating that she knew she had won the argument.

Thran built a pile of twigs and leaves near the cave entrance. He smacked two rocks together, generated a spark, blew on it, and produced a small but satisfying blaze.

The hearts of two 21st century humans soared.

"For a long time, I have been looking for a way to cut hair," said Thran. His hair was, in fact, so long that he was in danger of tripping over it. He used the fire to light a torch. He applied the torch flame to the ends of his hair. The fire quickly engulfed all of his hair, and he ran screaming from the cave.

"That's Thran for you," said the apparently female

shaggy person. "Always showing off."

The reporters raced after him. As Thran leapt into a stream, another shaggy person approached, carrying several small animal carcasses. The hunter built a fire on a level, sandy spot about 100 feet away and started to cook the animals. The journalists inched forward so their viewers could get a closer view.

Deidre reached out an arm to restrain her partner. Wade soon realized why. There was movement in some nearby bushes, despite the absence of wind.

Two lions sprang from the bushes and raced toward the fire. One landed on the hunter. The other went for the hunter's dinner. The sounds were horrifying. Deidre and Wade crouched in their tracks, motionless and silent, for fear of becoming dessert. Eventually, the lions finished eating and wandered off.

Deidre was trembling and speechless. Wade could manage only: "It's a jungle out here."

Thran returned, his head scorched and bleeding. He passed the reporters without speaking to them, stopped at the base of his hill, let loose a shrill whistle, and shouted: "Fellow shaggy people: Misery and death accompany these two strangers. They must be witches. We must burn them."

Shaggy people emerged from previously unnoticed caves and poured down the hillside toward the reporters.

"Bess is disguised as a large boulder this time," Wade reminded Deidre.

"Yes, but which one?" croaked Deidre, who appeared to be on the verge of bursting into tears. Wade had never seen his partner lose her cool. It was almost charming.

Wade did a quick 360. "That pale brown boulder, with the wavy ridge along the front. I remember it because the ridge is shaped like my hairline."

Wade took Deidre's hand and led her briskly toward the time machine. But just before they could reach it, two shaggy people grabbed her. Wade spun, his right fist connecting with the head of one of the shaggy people and his right leg delivering a serious blow below the belt—that is, below where a belt would be if the second shaggy person had a belt.

Both shaggy people collapsed, moaning. Wade found the door, shoved Deidre into the time machine, and dove in after her. Bess hit the proverbial gas to take them home.

For a few moments, no one spoke. Then Deidre leaned close to Wade and reached out an arm as if to embrace him. At the last instant she froze, then patted him on the shoulder and stated in a formal voice: "Thank you."

A BIG CITY; PRESENT DAY

Chris fought his way to the front of the small mob pressed against the reception desk in the lobby of the Hysteria Channel building, elbowing aside people dressed in Star Wars and Star Trek costumes, people adorned with tin foil hats and space alien masks, all manner of kooks insisting— like Chris—that they absolutely had to talk to the reporters of "Yore Right". The visitors wanted to travel to the future, to the past, to other planets and galaxies. Many of them claimed that the fate of the universe depended upon them.

Of course, Chris just had to say it: "The fate of the universe depends upon me."

Fred Finta, who was working the desk, wondered for the ninety-ninth time that morning whether he had made the right career choice. He told Chris: "If it's so important, why don't you just beam yourself up?"

"Good idea," conceded Chris. "But I didn't bring the proper equipment with me."

"It's a mystery to me," said Tony, leaning on the conference room table. "Somehow, you three dimwits managed to create the two highest-rated shows ever broadcast on the Hysteria Channel. But we have to keep producing must-see episodes if we want to turn this network around."

Wade and Eddie smiled; Deidre was too astonished to consider taking any credit.

"I'm not going anywhere where they try to run us over or eat us or burn us," she told Tony. "We could have been killed."

"I know. That would have been so bloody spectacular," he said. "But the first two shows were a little too…complicated."

"Why don't we do an episode in the future? Everybody will want to see that," offered Wade.

Eddie spoke up. "I've taken Bess to do some scouting in the future. Man, it's depressing with a capital D."

"How so?" Deidre inquired.

"Well, you have your close encounters with killer asteroids. There's a bunch of pandemics. And, a nasty alien invasion that sets off World War XVII."

"There really will be seventeen world wars?" asked Wade.

"No, only sixteen that we know of. Everyone got together and agreed to skip number thirteen, because it would be unlucky."

"Makes sense," said Tony.

"Hold the elevator," pleaded Wade. For once, the request worked.

The door closed. He was alone with Deidre as they headed to the ground floor. They had only a few minutes before the start of episode three.

"About that last episode," began Deidre.

Wade studied her eyes, then moved closer to her. He leaned in, watching to see if she would pull away if he tried to kiss her. She didn't, so he put his hands on her shoulders and planted a wet one. He drew back, expecting a slap. Instead, Deidre stared at him intensely for a moment, then pulled him close and locked fiercely onto his lips, tongue, tonsils, and anything else she could reach.

The elevator door opened on the second floor. Eddie entered with a handful of snacks.

The reporters moved apart nervously and adjusted their clothing. Eddie seemed oblivious or indifferent to what he had witnessed.

"Germany. 1511. Pretty cool, huh?" said Eddie.

GERMANY; 16TH CENTURY

"Cute little town," Eddie observed as he and the reporters surveyed the prosperous-looking village that had materialized beyond the time machine's windows.

Said Bess: "The house on the right with the brown shutters is the one where Peter Henlein lives. I will remain in this shaded corner of the town square disguised as a schnitzel delivery wagon."

As Deidre and Wade approached the house, a woman screamed "Behold!" extremely loud and at close range. The reporters jumped involuntarily and looked around to determine what was going on. The few locals passing through the square paid the noise no mind. Wade knocked on Peter's door, and he and Deidre were welcomed into a foyer and then to a second-floor workshop cluttered with boxes and springs and gears of various sizes and shapes.

"We understand that you are inventing a clock," began Wade. He felt silly in the outfit that Bess was projecting for him, which consisted of puffy sleeves, tight britches, and a wide, flat hat.

"I am trying," said Peter, a small man with a dark beard, moustache, and receding hairline. "Excuse me one moment." He stuck his right arm out a window and noted the position of the sun's shadow on the small sundial he wore on his wrist. Then he returned to his workbench and made an adjustment to his invention.

Another "Behold!" rumbled across the square.

"Can you tell us how it works?" said Deidre, who was virtually outfitted in a long blue woolen petticoat with violet trim. Her hair was tied back in a bun, creating a matronly image that nearly caused Wade to break out laughing every time he looked at her.

"You see these gears?" said Peter. "They—"

"Behold!"

"As I was saying, the gears connect with the pendulum, and the mainspring—"

"Behold!" And another "Behold!"

Peter grimaced. "I am sorry about those women. They are the town criers. They are all supposed to sing precisely at the start of each minute, using this new musical form, which we call opera. But they are not—"

"Behold!"

"They are not coordinated. They cannot use sundials because they are seated inside the church tower, so they try to keep time by watching candles melt."

Said Wade: "When will your new clock—"

"Behold!"

Deidre gasped. "Wade, your hair!"

"I know, it's great, but let's focus on Peter."

"No, your hair, and your clothes. They're...normal."

Gone were the puffy sleeves, tight britches, and flat hat. Instead, everyone in the room could see the Ohio State sweatshirt, jeans and tennis shoes that he had put on this morning. Deidre's outfit had reverted to a white blouse, navy slacks and stylish but comfortable 21st century shoes. And, the journalists surmised, their words were now coming across to Peter in English, not German.

Peter just stared.

Policeman Nikolas Beber considered it his job to know everyone in town. Everyone, and their work. Everyone, and their possessions. Everyone, and their deepest, darkest secrets. The town was, on the whole, free of crime. Sure, a few youngsters skipped school now and then; Nikolas could be counted on to treat them to a brief but memorable dose of corporal punishment. But he had a lot of time on his hands.

As he was rather portly, Nicholas managed his morning rounds at a leisurely pace. But as soon as he reached the town square, he sensed that something was not normal. There, in the shade. He approached the apparently unlicensed schnitzel delivery wagon and prepared to holler "Whose wagon might this be?" But as the first syllable left his lips, he was drowned out by a booming "Behold!"

He decided to apply his investigative powers. Which, for Nikolas, consisted of sticking out his hand and removing the cover from the wagon. Or, it would have consisted of this specific action, had there been an actual cover and an actual wagon. Instead, his hand disappeared through the three-dimensional projection of a cover and encountered empty air.

Inside the time machine, Eddie sat paralyzed with terror. "Bess, what should we do?"

"I compute a high probability that this man will continue to ignore the illusion of the delivery wagon and will make contact with our transport vehicle. That would be unfortunate. It would be even more unfortunate if he were to enter the vehicle."

On cue, Nikolas probed the side of the "wagon" and touched a glass window. He pulled back his hand, uttered a mild curse, then gathered his courage and reached out once more. This time, he encountered metal. His fingers found what felt like a hinge, and he lifted it.

Eddie grasped the door handle from the inside and pulled, matching the policeman's effort. But Eddie was not particularly strong, and it was evident to him that the policeman would soon manage to open the door.

"Bess, get us out of here," he whispered.

"Are you sure this is what you want? What about Deidre and Wade?"

"We'll have to come back for them."

The door opened an inch. Two more. Then, abruptly, the exterior pressure on the door handle ceased, and Eddie pulled the door shut. It was dark outside, but a partial moon shed enough light to reveal that they were in a pasture.

"Thanks, Bess. I sure hope they're okay."

"Let me explain," said Deidre, but the confused expression on Peter's face confirmed that her words were no longer coming across to him in German. She had studied the language in high school and college, so she switched to speaking it. "We are...actors. Yes, actors. We travel with strange clothes, and..."

She glanced at Wade, who was smiling nervously and trying to pretend that everything was fine.

"...and I think we have taken enough of your time," continued Deidre. "Wade, why don't we leave and let this great inventor get back to his work."

She motioned to Wade to rise, and they headed for the stairs.

"Just a moment," said Peter, freezing Deidre in her tracks. "Why did you refer to me as a great inventor?"

"We have a feeling that your clock will be important. It will be something historic, something that will help many people," said Deidre.

Peter closed his eyes and sighed. "It warms my heart to hear you say that. All these years, no one has given me much encouragement." He stood and shook Wade's hand. Then he lifted Deidre's and kissed it gently. "You theater people are unusual. But so are those of us who try to create something new. I wish you success."

As the reporters descended the stairs, Wade whispered: "What the hell?"

"Something must have happened to Bess," said Deidre.

Opening the front door, they were confronted by a small but energetic crowd that had gathered in front of Peter's house. The locals started shaking signs reading "No Clocks" and "Save the Singers". One shouted that the town criers would go on strike if Peter persisted with his invention.

Gradually, silence descended as the crowd scrutinized clothing never before seen or conceived in the town.

"What manner of dress is this?" demanded one of the women. "Are you friends of the inventor?"

Deidre said something very rude under her breath.

Wade started jumping up and down and waving his arms like a madman. To Deidre he said: "Run! Get out of here. I'll think of something." Then Wade plunged into the throng, shouting random phrases in English such as "Stairway to heaven!" and "I am the walrus!"

Deidre ducked into a nearby alley, crouching behind a pile of trash and peeking out every few seconds. A couple of older women started beating Wade with their protest signs. "Not the hair!" Wade yelled in vain. "Please, don't mess up my hair!"

Across the square, Nikolas continued to walk over and around the spot where some sort of wagon had stood just moments earlier. He paced and stared, still not comprehending what had transpired. He might have lingered there all day had not a small riot broken out nearby. Still reeling, he meandered over to the crowd and broke up the conflict before anyone could inflict any permanent damage on Wade's fabulous follicles.

"Who are you, sir, and what are you doing in my town?" the policeman demanded.

Wade could only guess what the man was asking and

could only hope that he understood English. "I am sorry. I am lost and need help."

To Nikolas, who spoke no English, Wade might as well have been saying: "I am a monster here to steal your women and rape your livestock."

Nikolas ordered the demonstrators to go home. Then, with immense satisfaction, he dragged Wade off to jail.

Deidre tried to formulate a plan. Her first task was to remain hidden, and she was thankful that none of the dispersing protesters had passed through the alley where she was holed up. She crept back into the square just long enough to confirm that the time machine was not where she and Wade had left it.

Deidre needed a period-appropriate outfit. She looked for a clothesline. Only children's items were drying in her alley. Turning a corner, she found several adult petticoats like the one Bess had projected for her, hanging on a line. She snatched a pale pink outfit and took a couple of steps.

"Ahem."

Deidre turned to face a rather plump woman who was holding a rather large rolling pin. "I don't believe that belongs to you."

"It fell. I was just going to shake the dust off of it and put it back," Deidre said. She tried to supplement her rusty German with a smile. She didn't think it was working. She was right.

"Inside," ordered the woman. "Now!"

Deidre had no choice but to comply.

It was a large, well-appointed house. The occupants were surely well-to-do. Maybe they would not be too upset about a little petty coat larceny, thought Deidre. The woman motioned for her to sit at the kitchen table.

"You are new in town, correct?"

"Yes."

"Why are you dressed like that?"

Deidre considered repeating the line about being an actor. She didn't think it would work. She racked her brain for a better response.

"And why do you speak with such an odd accent?" the woman inquired. It seemed that she was more curious than angry.

"I am so, so sorry," said Deidre, as obsequiously as she could manage. "It was a stupid, thoughtless thing to do. I pray that you can find it in your heart to forgive me."

The woman eyed Deidre intensely. Then she rose and started to make tea. Neither woman spoke until the warm liquid infused Deidre with a sense of hope.

"I have heard tales of people wearing strange clothing and speaking with odd accents," the woman stated. "To my knowledge, I have never encountered someone who was raised by wolves. By any chance, was that your fate?"

Deidre struggled to process the question without revealing her astonishment.

"Yes, you have learned my secret," Deidre confessed. "I am so ashamed."

"Oh, you poor girl," said the woman, leaving her seat and giving Deidre a hug that nearly squeezed the life out of her. After a few moments: "Do you have anywhere to stay?"

"No. I am lost. And hungry. And scared."

"You won't be scared any longer, my dear. You are going to stay here, as long as you wish. My brother is a priest, and as a man of God he surely will agree with me. Now, let's get you cleaned up and fed."

Deidre began to shed tears, without having to fake them. "I am so, so grateful," she said. "I have never had a real home before."

"My name is Katherine," the woman stated.

"Deidre."

As Katherine led Deidre through the house, Deidre oohed and ahhed at the size of the rooms and the luxurious furnishings. When they got to the top of the stairs, Deidre said: "There is one more thing. My brother, who I have been responsible for my whole life, was just taken away by a policeman. He must be terribly scared and worried about me.

Is there any way that we can help him, too?"

Katherine's smile darkened. "I am not sure what we can do about that, dearie."

The sun was directly overhead when Bess manifested in a wooded area on the edge of town. She was disguised this time as a huge old tree with red flowers so Eddie could find her easily after retrieving the reporters.

"Be careful," she told Eddie. "It's almost 300 yards from here to Peter Henlein's house. If you go much further, you'll be exposed."

"Here goes nothing," said Eddie as he exited. He bowed to a couple of people he passed. As he reached the house that Deidre and Wade had entered, he noticed that the shutters were green, not brown. He knocked anyway. A woman answered the door.

"Excuse me, is Peter here?"

"No one named Peter lives here. What do you want?"

"Sorry. My mistake. Have a nice day."

Eddie found the flowering tree, entered the time machine, and told Bess what had transpired.

"We must have returned sometime before or after Peter lived there. I apologize for my error," said Bess. "I will try again."

This time, the time machine materialized at dusk on a farm.

"Bess, are you okay?"

"I don't know. I will run some diagnostics. I must be experiencing something like what you humans call jet lag."

"Can I help?"

"Thank you for your kind offer, Eddie. I do not think that there is anything you can do."

A BIG CITY; PRESENT DAY

After six failed attempts to return to the right town at the right time, Bess managed to limp into the Hysteria Channel parking lot four days after Eddie and the reporters had embarked on episode three. Sheepishly, Eddie knocked on Tony's office door.

"It's about time," said Tony. "What happened out there?"

Eddie explained what little he knew.

"That episode was a real stinker," Tony said. "People were running away from it like it was a crazed skunk with the clap and an AK-47. The only blessing was that the video and audio signal from Bess went dead while the reporters were yakking with that boring clockmaker. We can't afford another disaster like that."

"Did you hear me say that we lost Deidre and Wade?"

"Yes. So?"

"Well, I want to rescue them."

"You couldn't rescue a cat from a canary," said Tony. "Besides, reporters are a dime a dozen. You ever hear an editor refer to a writer as his prize reporter?"

"I guess so."

"Well, that means the editor is planning to give him away."

Eddie gave Tony a blank stare.

"Listen, kid; I'm glad you and Bess are back, blah blah blah. But things are really bad here. We all might lose our jobs, and I have no retirement plan. All we have is a senile time machine. I think we ought to make a bundle of money fast and move to Aruba. Got any ideas?"

"There's a lot of artificial plants in office buildings around here. We could start selling artificial water for people to use with them."

"Interesting, but the business would take too long to ramp up."

"We could go back in time a few years and buy a bunch of Microsoft and Apple stock."

"If the taxes don't kill us, we'll probably get nailed for insider trading. How about this: We go forward a couple of days and learn what the next winning lottery numbers will be."

A man who neither Tony nor Eddie recognized entered the room, took a seat, and said: "Greetings. I come in peace."

"Who the hell are you?" asked Tony.

"I am Chris. I have come to take back my time machine."

"How did you get in here?"

"I told the receptionist that I am a contestant on 'Celebrity Stalker'."

"Which episode?"

"That was an inaccurate statement on my part, for which I apologize. But the time machine really is mine. Well, not mine personally, but I was the one who brought it here."

"Prove it. What's its nickname?"

"Bess."

"Could be a lucky guess. Assuming for the sake of argument that you are from the future, why did you come here?"

"I am a maintenance tech for temporal transport devices. We had a report of problems with one unit, so I took it out on a test run. I chose this place and time because I have been absolutely dying to try a pastrami on rye sandwich from the deli on 16th Street, which Bess recommended highly. You see, in my time, no one eats real meat anymore. Much of the food tastes like quinoa that's been pummeled by days of acid rain, because that's what it is. But I couldn't find the deli. While I was away from the machine, one of you must have discovered it and given it a new disguise."

"The deli's owners retired about a month ago. It was replaced by a marijuana shop," said Eddie. "I hear that the brownies are amazing."

"That explains my problem. But it also reinforces my concern that Bess might be malfunctioning."

"Well, she's the best time machine I've ever used," said Tony. "If you really are from the future, tell us something that's going to happen to us. Like, when will I be rich and famous?"

"If I told you your futures, it would make you miserable," said Chris. "Who wants to know when they are going to get fired or get hit by a truck?"

"Bummer," said Eddie.

"I can tell you this," said Chris. "There are massively powerful AIs in my time, and no governments. Everyone has cybernetic enhancements to their brains and bodies, and the sex…"

Eyebrows raised.

"We use time machines to learn from the past," Chris continued. "But there are still a few things that have been puzzling some of us, and maybe you can help clear up one of them. There's a person called Kim Kardashian—someone born in your time, I believe. She has had thousands of regeneration and cybernetic enhancement procedures. But no one can seem to recall her purpose. Does she have any special talent or reason for being kept alive all these centuries?"

Heads shook in bafflement.

"Anyway," said Chris, "you'll be glad to know that Tom Brady is still slinging footballs as far as ever. And Brett Favre is considering another comeback."

"That doesn't do us any good," replied Tony. All of a sudden, his eyes looked like they were about to explode out of his head. "I've got it. We'll go back in time to the formation of CNN so we can sabotage it. That would give the Hysteria Channel its best chance to survive."

"Time travel machines are not toys. You can do irreparable damage if you are not cautious," advised Chris.

Tony stared him down. "Wait a minute. You came looking for a deli that isn't here, lost a time machine, and are telling *us* to be careful?"

Chris hung his head. "Okay, I messed up. I just can't believe that anyone would bother with a food truck purporting to offer cuisine from Easter Island. What do they eat there? Rocks?"

"So, there is an Easter Island?" asked Eddie.

"Speaking of mistakes," said Chris, "it appears that something went wrong on the latest episode of 'Yore Right'. Did your reporters return safely?"

"They're on a sabbatical," Tony said, "at whatever salary they can earn back in 16th century Germany."

"That's terrible," said Chris. "It's terrible for them, and it's worse for temporal continuity. This could change history in so many ways—so many unpredictable and potentially disastrous ways."

"Not my problem."

"There's one more thing you should know," said Chris. "Traveling to one's future is absolutely prohibited."

"Oops," said Eddie, who decided to change the subject. "Chris, could you help me and Bess rescue Deidre and

Wade?"

"Out of the question," barked Tony.

"I would be glad to do so," said Chris. "And it would be good for your ratings, Tony. Everyone loves a happy ending."

"Have you ever watched the Hysteria Channel?"

"If you let Eddie, Bess, and myself secure the reporters, when we return, I will help you save your network."

Tony appeared to be softening his opposition. "So, you and Eddie would represent the so-called talent on this episode? God help us."

"You won't have to pay me, if that makes you feel better. Eddie, are you ready?"

"We have to do a burger run first," he said. "I haven't eaten in, like, 500 years."

EVERYWHERE

The second disruption to the space-time fabric got just about everyone's attention.

For most people, it started as a feeling that everything was slowing down, like a special effect in a movie. It didn't last long.

But it was totally weird.

Remember that funhouse mirror trick where you stood in the right place and saw countless copies of yourself streaming into infinity? This phenomenon was something like that, except that in one direction were versions of you in decreasing age, and in the other direction were variations of you who were older and older.

You couldn't focus well on them, especially the ones farthest in the past and future, but for a moment, one or two of them might have shocked you right out of your socks.

The phenomenon caused some mishaps. A young woman trying to make a sundae in a Chicago suburb sent whipped cream flying in all directions except on top of the ice cream. Some couples making love wondered if they had been joined by uninvited participants. A number of young people on the West Coast and in desert communes responded with a "Far out!" Many religious leaders described it as a Sign From Above, though they disagreed what the message might be. A few folks chalked it up to bad sushi. In New York City, it was shrugged off by most people without a second thought.

Tony saw himself in that ridiculous bright blue suit, the one he absolutely hated. But ITV was paying him and insisted that he wear it, so he wore it.

How long ago was it? One year? Thirty? He couldn't think straight. As the images faded, he reflected on his career path and the personal choices that he had made—and that had been made for him—along the way.

Tony had tried to be a good husband. But he wasn't rich enough, wasn't dashing enough, and wasn't focused enough on Mabel for her liking. They fought constantly, even more so when he got the game show gig. Now he was a minor celebrity, and she was no longer the center of his life. Then came the affairs. When they finally got around to getting divorced, it was an anticlimax. It had been over for a long time, maybe even from the start.

But that blue suit. How it shone under those TV lights. What was the name of the show? "Who Wants—" Oh yes, "Who Wants to Be a Pauper?" The producers kept finding these rich Brits willing to go on TV and answer trivia questions. Each correct answer cost them money, starting with a thousand pounds and cascading up to as much as 256 grand. The best part was that Tony got to insult the contestants—the ones who failed, and the ones who got the answers right. He absolutely shed saliva when pronouncing "twit". The audience loved it.

However, the divorce and the bright lights took a toll

on Tony. His insults became more bitter. His hairline receded, and his waist grew. The ratings dropped. One day, without warning, he was sacked. He woke up in a gutter with a hangover. Nothing for it but to leave for America and start over.

At least he never had to wear that ghastly blue suit again.

Nikolas had just ordered Wade to strip when it hit. The policeman stumbled, then crawled out the jailhouse door. Wade stood there in his boxers as the figures from his past and future fanned out in opposite directions.

The one shining brightest was out toward one end. He squinted and saw what appeared to be a man stooped over and using a cane to get around. The man was clearly old and decrepit. And bald. Completely, horrifically bald.

That can't be me, thought Wade. *That can never happen to me. I will get hair plugs, endure transplants, swallow bottles of pills, whatever it takes. I will take a full head of hair to my grave.*

There was something else about that figure, now completely faded. Wade couldn't quite grasp it, like the faint wisps of a departing dream. He started thinking about what life was like back in high school in Toledo. He saw himself trying to get a date with an older cheerleader. He saw himself getting turned down, by her and other girls, again and again. He was a geek with a crew cut back then. He played sports, and he was starting to get good at baseball and golf, but he was one of the least popular kids in the whole school. He cried himself to sleep every night, and he felt ashamed. He vowed that he would become really popular, no matter what it took.

Suddenly, Wade remembered that last impression from the old man who might be his future self. That man was not alone. There was a someone else there. A woman. A tall woman with dark hair.

Nikolas returned and handed Wade a gunny sack. "Wear this."

Eddie and Chris were waiting for their burgers when the ripple struck.

The figure in Eddie's past that stood out to him seemed to be holding something, something cold and inviting, perhaps a bowl of ice cream.

That would have been when he was nine years old. That would have been before he and his mom moved to that small apartment.

His mom had come in the front door of their house without her usual cheery welcome. She turned off the TV and asked him to follow her into the kitchen. She filled a bowl with strawberry ice cream and handed it to Eddie and took a seat next to him. It was then that he noticed that her eyes were red.

There was a robbery at the bank where your father works, she told him. Your father was very brave. He tried to stop the robber. He tried to protect other people from being hurt by the robber. The robber was a bad man. He... There were gunshots. Three people...died.

Eddie knew that his dad was gone.

Strawberry is the only flavor of ice cream that Eddie won't eat.

Chris was almost as excited as Eddie while they waited for their food. It wasn't pastrami on rye, but a real hamburger— no, a real cheeseburger...

As the unexpected images spread through his consciousness, he felt a surge of adrenaline, a peak of emotion, a twinge of guilt. Somewhere among those possible futures, there was a Chris who would be held accountable for what he had started by taking the trip searching for that deli. This phenomenon could be a manifestation of his mistakes. Perhaps one of many side effects.

For what? A pastrami on rye sandwich. For that, he put so many people at such great risk.

He felt like crying, like begging for forgiveness. He wanted to fast-forward to his judgment day. Tell me my crime, give me my punishment, and let me atone. Would he be scolded by the AIs? Would he be transferred to another job? Would he be allowed to do anything productive?

When the human figures faded, he felt empty. But after a few moments, he realized that he had a purpose. He would help the people he had met, the people whose lives he had impacted. He would prove his worth. And, after he had done everything that he could do, he would tell the AIs: I'm only human.

"Am I dreaming?" Deidre asked herself. She was in bed when the vision appeared, with so many figures heading off in both directions, all apparently female.

All except one.

He was an inch or two shorter than she was. He had a pleasant face, an intelligent face. He was young. And he was smiling at her, obviously pleased to be looking at her.

The vision faded.

He looked nothing like Richard. Richard, the only boy she had ever dated seriously. Yes, he was a boy, not a man. While she had been only in her early twenties at the time, she was always mature for her years.

Even during her childhood, she shunned silly games and silly girls. She did not date in high school, except for a group date to her prom. In college, Richard had refused to take no for an answer and wore her down until she agreed to go out with him. She dated him for two years. She refused to sleep with him, yet he kept trying to get past her resistance. He said he loved her. He even hinted that he would marry her if she would just loosen up. Because of his overbearing nature, it was easy to break up with him.

No, the man in her vision was nothing like Richard. And that bothered Deidre.

EARTH; FAR, FAR FUTURE

A time-quake, observed the RRRRBAI. Not merely a ripple or minor disturbance, but the genuine article. He knew that they were theoretically possible. But he had never experienced a full-blown time-quake. Or, if he had, he'd forgotten it. No, that couldn't be right. He couldn't forget or be unaware of such a momentous, ominous occurrence.

After all, he was an RRRRBAI, a Really, Really, Really, Really Big Artificial Intelligence.

A BIG CITY/GERMANY

"You can do this, Bess. Just concentrate." Chris believed in his heart that she could still travel from the crowded Hysteria Channel parking lot to any time and place that a human required.

She had to. Because, if she did not, people would be stuck in times and places they never intended to be stuck. And it would be his fault.

"Try to visualize the town square and the house where Peter Henlein lives," continued Chris.

"And the women's voices singing 'Behold!'," added Eddie. "And the smell of sausages in the air. Really pungent sausage smells. Sausages that you can almost taste, sausages that—"

"I get it," said Bess, politely. "I will do my best."

On the first try, they wound up in some sort of swamp. On the second go: the right town but in the early Middle Ages. For the third foray: the side of a modern superhighway. Fourth journey: success. Bess was once again disguised as a tree with red flowers on the edge of the German village. It was morning.

"I think you did it, Bess. I knew you could," said Eddie.

"Thank you. Your support means a lot to me."

Eddie sat up straight and smiled. "Welcome to episode four of 'Yore Right.' I am Eddie. Chris and I are going to rescue Deidre and Wade back in 15th century Germany."

"It's the 16th century," noted Chris.

"No. It's the year 1511, so it's the 15th century."

Chris didn't want to get into a long explanation and embarrass Eddie on live TV. "Sorry, my mistake."

The men made sure that no one was watching before they exited the time machine. They did double-takes as they checked out the clothes Bess had projected for them. "We could almost be brothers," observed Eddie.

"Sure," said Chris, with zero conviction.

The house had brown shutters once again, and the protesters had returned. Chris and Eddie moved cautiously past the locals and knocked on the door. Peter welcomed them into his workshop.

"It is so unusual to have all these visitors," he stated. "You are the second pair of strangers to come look at my invention this very week."

"How is it coming?" asked Eddie.

"Very—"

A "Behold!" shook windows.

"I'm sure it will be a huge success," said Chris. "Do you happen to know the whereabouts of our two friends, the people who came to visit you earlier?"

"A man and an attractive young woman?"

"Yes, that's them."

"It would be difficult to forget them. They spoke two languages and changed clothes as quickly as you can snap your fingers," he said. "There was some commotion when they left this house. I do not know where the woman went. But the man was taken away by the policeman."

"Thank you for—"

"Behold!"

Chris and Eddie took that as their cue to move on.

The first three passersby refused to cooperate when Chris and Eddie tried to get directions to the town jail. The fourth listened, pointed and said she hoped that they found their stay there a lengthy one.

"I thought small towns were friendly," said Chris as they reached their destination. "This could be harder than I thought. Perhaps you should let me handle this."

Upon opening the jailhouse door, they discovered a man with his feet propped up on an ancient wooden desk. Eddie recognized him as the policeman who had tried to gain entry to the time machine on their first visit to town. Behind the policeman were two cells. Two older men who appeared to be sleeping off a bender occupied the one on the left. A man attired in what appeared to be a gunny sack napped in the right-hand cell. The hair was an instant giveaway: Wade.

Eddie whispered to Chris: "That's him."

Nikolas removed his feet from the desk slowly and eyed the strangers suspiciously. "Who the hell are you?"

"We have come to claim your prisoner. The one on the right," said Chris in an officious tone.

"By what authority?"

"He is a wanted man. A dangerous man," continued Chris. "A man you don't want in your town. We will be glad to take him off your hands and bring him to justice."

"Again: By what authority?"

Chris looked down at the floor and pondered his next move. This was a lot harder than he anticipated.

Eddie straightened up, took several steps forward, leaned over the desk and stuck out his chin. "Perhaps you don't know who we are," he stated.

Chris was tempted to grab Eddie and drag him out of the building, but he was curious to see what Eddie had in mind.

"We represent the Spanish Inquisition," said Eddie.

"Yes, the Spanish Inquisition!" He heaved his chest slightly, trying to look imposing and hoping to convince himself that he could keep this schtick going.

"The Spanish Inquisition? I did not expect anyone representing the Spanish Inquisition."

"Ha!" responded Eddie, so loudly that he woke Wade. "Nobody expects the Spanish Inquisition!"

Eddie paused, not sure what to say next. It had been a while since he had streamed "Monty Python."

The policeman frowned. "You don't look like cardinals."

"We are undercover," said Eddie. "So…so no one will expect us. Right. If you don't believe us, phone the Vatican."

"Phone?"

"I mean, imagine how the Vatican would react if you refused to do our bidding."

"Yeah, imagine," Wade chipped in sarcastically.

The only thing on Chris's mind was the wish that he had brought some spare undergarments on this outing.

Eddie walked casually to Wade's cell and rested his left arm against the bars. "What charge do you place against this man?"

"Disturbing the peace."

A couple of "Behold!"s rattled the jailhouse.

"What peace?" said Eddie. "Listen to that racket." He was almost out of ideas.

"Look!" he exclaimed, pointing. "That big rat in the corner. It might be carrying the black plague!"

"What rat?" said the policeman.

Eddie used the distraction to remove a key from a wall hook and open Wade's cell.

"Time to run," said Chris, emerging from his torpor.

The pudgy policeman got to his feet slowly. The three visitors had a slight head start.

"Stick with me," Eddie told Wade as they burst out of the building. "Chris, you go left, we'll go right, and we'll rendezvous at the—"

"Shh," said Chris.

The policeman emerged from the jailhouse with a massive sword that appeared to be some sort of ceremonial weapon. Were it not so heavy, he might have sliced one of the three men in half. Were it not so heavy, he might have been able to keep up with Eddie and Wade as he chased them around the town square and through side streets. But Nikolas knew the town better than anyone, and he managed to herd the two fugitives into a dead end.

As he closed in on them, he took note of Eddie's attire. Eddie was outfitted in the style of clothes that Wade had been wearing when the policeman had arrested him.

"What manner of sorcery is this?" he shouted.

Wade and Eddie kept looking for an exit and failing to find one.

Nikolas grasped his sword with both hands and raised it over his head in a threatening manner. Then he cried out something very naughty and collapsed on the ground, doubled over in pain.

"He must have pulled something," said Eddie. "Let's go help him."

Eddie's frilly sleeves, tight britches and flat hat reappeared as he and Wade approached Nicholas. Each grabbed an arm. With their assistance, the policeman limped, groaning, all the way back to the jailhouse.

"The Spanish Inquisition? Where did that doozy come from?" Wade asked Eddie when they reached the time machine.

"My mom and I watch a lot of TV," responded Eddie. "I don't have many friends."

"Well, nice work. But what happened earlier while Deidre and I were talking to Peter Henlein?"

"The policeman noticed the time machine and tried to get inside. We had to leave. We thought we would come right back, but Bess got sort of lost. Did they feed you well in jail?"

"All the schnitzel I could eat."

Chris joined them in the machine, bearing a gift in the form of damp but wearable men's clothes pilfered from a window ledge to replace the sack on Wade's back.

"Thanks," said Wade. "But who the hell are you?"

"I'm Chris. You can thank me—or blame me—for bringing Bess to the 21st century."

"I won't blame you, as long as we can rescue Deidre and blow this crummy town."

"You will have to hurry if you want to rescue her," said Bess. "My programing limits each time travel event to two hours. Beyond that, I can no longer project disguises for you or for myself, or translate your speech. The intent of my programmers was to ensure that no time traveler was tempted to interact with the external environment."

"Like we have been doing almost nonstop," observed Chris.

"Correct."

"I'll be quick," said Wade.

He sprinted to Peter's house. The late afternoon sun streamed through the workshop window, igniting fiery sparks of light on the edges of metal scraps here and there.

"I take it your friends got you away from Nikolas Beber," said the inventor.

"Yes, and thanks for your help," said Wade. "Do you have any suggestions where I might look for my other colleague, Deidre?"

"Unfortunately, no. After you were taken away, the crowd dispersed, and I did not see her again. Now, let me ask you something. Who are you people?"

"That's a fair question. I'm not sure how best to answer you. It's important that I be, well, discreet, for reasons that I cannot tell you without causing a lot of trouble for a lot of people." He was grateful that he was no longer wearing a miniature camera or microphone.

"You do not seem like a criminal. But you are

obviously not from around here."

"Yes, all four of us come from far away. And I need to find Deidre and bring her back with us." He struggled with how much to tell Peter.

"You're a man of science," Wade continued. "So, I am going to be honest with you and am going to beg you never to tell another soul what I am about to say."

"I live alone. Your secret will be safe with me."

"We come from the New World. Christopher Columbus thought that he would find a western route to India, but he actually discovered a new continent."

"Really? Go on."

As if on cue: "Behold!"

"Here's the amazing part: We come from five hundred years in your future."

Peter sat back and studied Wade.

"You seem like a crazy man at times," Peter said. "But not at this moment. How is what you are claiming possible?"

"Chris is a man from my future. He brought a time travel machine into our lives in the 21st century. While using it, Deidre and I became trapped accidentally in this time and place. My friends came back for me, but I must depart now and will return when I can. Would you look for Deidre while I am away?"

"I will do whatever I can."

"Thank you. When you find her, tell her that I will come for her in the town square at noon on a Wednesday. I don't know which Wednesday. Your clock can help, so please finish it as soon as you can."

"I will expedite my work."

"One more thing," said Wade, rising to leave. "Tell her that I...that I..."

Peter smiled. "You can tell her when you see her."

During the first days after she became separated from Wade, Deidre had been allowed out of the house only once, for a brief shopping excursion with Katherine. The older woman kept a close eye on Deidre, who studied everything and everyone she encountered but said very little.

Then came Sunday. After breakfast, Deidre was presented with an expensive outfit and escorted to the church by Katherine and her brother, Father Johannes. The priest gave a long, rambling sermon about sin and eternal damnation. Deidre struggled to stay awake.

After the service, she walked out of the church with Katherine and the priest, both of whom halted just beyond the front door. Deidre's hosts talked endlessly with each neighbor as he or she exited. During one such chat, Deidre slipped away, found the jailhouse, and passed through the open door.

The policeman was nowhere to be seen. Two old men issued catcalls from one cell. The other cell was empty, with the door wide open.

"What trouble are you causing now, Wade?" she muttered.

By the time she returned to the church, the congregation was all but gone. Katherine could guess where Deidre had been, but she did not press the point.

"I would like to introduce you to someone," said Katherine with a big smile. "This is Konrad Adler. He is a university student with a very bright future."

Deidre was unable to mouth even a simple "how do you do". Konrad was the man she had seen in her vision.

Said Father Johannes, placing one arm on Konrad's shoulder and another on Deidre's, "I am sure that you two young people will get along very well."

A BIG CITY; CURRENT DAY

Eddie's mother had never seen a real TV camera or a real network reporter in person. Eddie had promised to give her a tour of the Hysteria Channel building one night when he was working the late shift, but they never got past the cafeteria.

So, it was startling to have CNN, ABC, Fox, and NBC correspondents and their camera operators sitting in her tiny living room. The doorbell kept ringing, but almost every seat in the room was occupied, and she was running out of Mountain Dew and Twinkies to serve her existing guests.

"Are you sure that you don't want something else to eat? Look at you, you're skin and bones," said Ethyl Corbin to the CNN reporter.

"No, nothing, thank you," said the correspondent, who had been the first to arrive and was angry that she had not gotten the exclusive interview she felt she deserved.

Finally, Ethyl sat.

"Your son is a celebrity," said the CNN reporter. "Tells us about him."

"My Eddie is not a celebrity. You must have him confused with someone else."

"Eddie Corbin is your son, right? The Eddie who works at the Hysteria Channel?"

"Yes, that's him. He works in maintenance."

Some of the reporters wondered if there could be two Eddies at the same network.

"Did you watch the latest episode of 'Yore Right'?"

"I planned to, but I dozed off."

"Your son is trying to rescue Wade Braun and Deidre Lucchesi in 16th century Germany. What is your reaction to his heroism?"

"The 16th century, you say? I don't think that is my Eddie. He doesn't go anywhere if they don't have fast food."

GERMANY; 16TH CENTURY

Bess's bad day was getting worse. "I fear that I have lost my ability to navigate accurately," she told Eddie, Wade, and Chris.

Said Eddie: "You mean we could all be stranded here in Germany?"

"We must leave this time and place soon, before my disguise lapses and we are discovered. And whatever our next destination turns out to be, it would also have to be temporary, for the same reason."

"Could we go someplace where you don't have to disguise yourself? Like out in the wilderness?"

"How would you live?"

"Right, no fast-food joints. Could we send an SOS back to the Hysteria Channel using the cameras and microphones Chris and I are wearing?"

"I doubt that the signal is still getting through to your time. But even if we could send a message, what could they do?"

Eddie removed the miniature cameras and mikes from the clothes he and Chris were wearing. Episode Four had started out as an adventure, but it had descended into a horror show.

"We have to fix Bess," said Chris. "She had some problems back in my era. Our travels might have impacted her abilities. And the strange phenomenon we all experienced could have done some damage as well."

Chris placed his hands over the dashboard. "Bess, I am going to take a look at your programming."

A BIG CITY; PRESENT DAY

"Let me put this in terms that even you can understand," said the Hysteria Channel vice president, jowls flapping every time he spoke. "We need more episodes of 'Yore Right', and we need them now. When will you air the next one?"

Tony's stomach was doing somersaults. He felt like two anvils were slamming rhythmically into the sides of his head. He wished for nothing more than that bottle of gin sitting in the bottom right drawer of his desk.

"Very soon," he said, crossing his fingers under the table. "The reporters and the time machine should be back at any moment."

He added mentally: *They damn well better be.*

GERMANY; 16TH CENTURY

Eddie and Wade sat on a fallen log in the woods while Chris tried to figure out what was wrong with Bess.

"We have to find Deidre," said Wade. "She will be expecting us on Wednesday. Or some Wednesday soon."

"Sounds good," said Eddie. "Wednesdays and Thursdays are my days off."

As night fell, Bess's disguise evaporated. Chris emerged from a magnificent glass-and-chrome time machine about the size of a compact car that was hovering above the forest floor.

"If we can get to the far, far future, the AIs should be able to fix her," he stated.

"You say 'if'," responded Wade. "Can we, or can't we?"

Chris dropped his voice to a whisper. "I can't tell if it's a hardware or software problem. Maybe both. But there's hope. Before I took Bess on my ill-fated trip to get that pastrami on rye, prior users had loaded a number of itineraries. Some of those subprograms seem to be intact. We might be able to use or alter that code. However, it will take some experimenting, and some luck."

"I thought going to the future was a no-no," said Eddie.

"It is. We can only hope that the AIs at that time recognize that this is our only option and show us mercy."

DEEP SPACE; DATE UNKNOWN

It was a desperate mission. The captain and crew, all volunteers, knew in advance that many of them would not live to see it succeed. But they all viewed it as essential to mankind's survival.

They hoped to establish the first permanent colony outside of Earth's solar system.

Before departure, the crew had been placed in suspension. Then the ship was flung across the cosmos at a fearsome speed by manipulating the mysteries of quantum physics. It slowed down near a large neutron star, and a slingshot maneuver propelled it toward a remote solar system. The crew members were reassembled by the ship's computers shortly before arrival at the destination. Ten of the reconstituted crew members wound up looking and acting like grape jelly and were excused from further duty, but six were revived successfully.

The second planet from the sun showed the most

promise: thin clouds, a moderate temperature, and a few shallow seas. It could become their new home, Captain Jane Howser told her five remaining crew members.

It was a small world. In more ways than one.

GERMANY/ITALY

"Bess, I'm starving. Can we go somewhere with lots of food? Lots of cheap food?"

"Wherever humans exist, there is food, Eddie."

"I feel better already."

It was apparent immediately that their new destination was loud and busy. Boisterous crowds were flowing down an avenue from right to left. Chris took note of their attire and glimpsed a famous structure; he knew instantly where Bess had taken them. Maybe a hundred yards away stood the Coliseum, in all of its glory.

"When in Rome…" observed Chris.

Eddie waited for him to complete his thought. "I give up. When in Rome, what?"

"When in Rome, food can't be far away," observed Wade. "Let's find some and come right back to the machine, so we can try again to get to the far, far future. Bess, what's your disguise here?"

"A manure wagon."

"Ewwww," said Eddie. "Do you have to do that?"

"Sorry, Eddie. I am mindful of the trouble we had in Germany when I was disguised as a schnitzel delivery wagon. This is the Roman version of the 1974 Ford Pinto. No one will come near it except you gentlemen."

Wade steeled himself. "Let's stick together." He opened the door and the three travelers found themselves dressed in white togas and sandals. There was much pushing and shoving. Chris nearly tripped over the uneven paving stones. The hustle and noise reminded Wade of a college football game.

"There should be food vendors in front of the building," shouted Chris. Before they knew it, the three men were swept down the avenue by the masses and into the Coliseum.

Just beyond the entrance, Chris and Wade corralled Eddie and pulled him to the side, free of the raging river of bodies. They could smell bread and meat and perhaps even fruit, but the scents were mixed with human sweat and animal odors, and the men were not sure where to look for sustenance.

"You three!" yelled a sizable man wearing a knee-length military uniform and leather boots. His metal helmet featured a tall red plume, and a nasty looking sword hung at his side. "Are you gladiators or clowns?"

It was obvious to whom the soldier was addressing his question.

"Glad—" began Eddie.

"Clowns," said Wade.

"Gladiator clowns," improvised Chris.

"Follow me."

The man was joined by three more soldiers, who hustled the time travelers down a poorly lit ramp to a lower level. The noise and smell were dreadful. Wade kept looking from side to side, as if there were some chance of escape. Eddie was grimacing. Chris seemed to be in shock.

They rounded a corner, passed under an archway, and

were shoved into a staging area, a sea of men and animals packed much too closely together. The only light came from a wide opening that led directly to the floor of the Coliseum. The crowd noise was a constant hum, punctuated by foot stomping, whistles, shouts, and occasional fights among patrons.

A roar swelled to a crescendo.

"That's probably the emperor arriving," said Chris. "That means it's showtime."

GERMANY; 16TH CENTURY

Deidre supposed that she shouldn't complain. She had her own room, a comfortable bed, lovely clothes, and three meals a day. Katherine treated her like the daughter she never had. And, while Deidre had only limited contact with Father Johannes, she was careful to thank him every day for allowing her to remain in his home.

But she wanted to know what happened to Bess, Eddie, and Wade. And she wanted to go home. She didn't put much hope in Wade's comment that he would "think of something", even if he had managed not to get tossed into the local jail. She wondered how he or Eddie would be able to find her.

At least once a day, Deidre invented an excuse to leave the house. She needed to buy some item for the evening meal. She wanted to find a nice present for the priest to thank him for hosting her. She sought fresh air and exercise. Invariably, Katherine would come up with a reason why such an excursion was not a good idea. Or, the older woman would decide to accompany Deidre, not letting her guest out of her sight.

On Thursday night, the priest invited Konrad to dinner. As Deidre feared, once the dishes were cleared away, Katherine and her brother retired, leaving the young people alone in the parlor. Deidre knew a setup when she saw one. And, in this case, she saw no escape.

ANCIENT ROME

Men and animals were forced out into the arena in groups. Terrible noise invariably followed. Occasionally, Wade, Eddie, and Chris could see figures fighting just outside the staging area. All the men returned on stretchers. Some looked like they might still be alive; many did not. Even some stricken animals were taken off the arena floor in carts and dumped near the trio.

Soldiers with pikes and other weapons barred escape.

"I just hate dying on an empty stomach," commented Eddie.

Wade was in no mood to offer sympathy. "Are you comfortable with your decision to describe us as gladiators?"

"It sounded cool at the time. Not so much now," said Eddie.

Four soldiers confronted the time travelers. "You three.

Move!"

They moved. Reluctantly. Then more energetically with pikes jabbed into their backs.

Brilliant sunshine and a surprising roar accompanied their emergence into the arena. Thousands of Romans hurled insults, and garbage, at the trio. In the center of the arena, about fifty yards from them, three very large human beings emerged from a red-and-silver-colored chariot. Cheers rose to ear-splitting levels as the men, in fancy gladiator raiment, waved to the crowd.

"You don't suppose we're meant to fight these brutes?" said Chris.

"I don't suppose. I know," said Wade. "It was nice meeting you. Well, actually, not so nice, to be honest."

"Fair enough."

Trumpets blared. The three gladiators charged toward their victims, brandishing large swords that gleamed brilliantly.

Chris really, really wished that he had brought some spare undergarments.

Wade picked up three pikes that apparently had been left for them to use. He figured that the weapons would delay death by only a few seconds, but what else was there to do? He handed one to each of his colleagues, gripped the third, and stepped in front of them.

"Spread out when they are about to hit us," said Wade.

"Then what?" asked Eddie.

"I don't know. I haven't thought beyond that."

When the gladiators came within spitting distance, the three visitors dropped their pikes and ran for their lives. They were met by a chorus of boos. The attackers split up, each marching steadily on his intended victim, anticipating the pleasure he would experience in consummating a dramatic kill.

Eddie had sprinted to the far side of the arena. There was an opening. But as he approached it, he discovered that it was blocked by heavily armed soldiers. He had about fifteen seconds to contemplate his next move as his assailant strode confidently toward him.

Chris ran in circles, clockwise, then counterclockwise. His would-be killer set the point of his sword into the dusty dirt near him and watched, laughing so hard that he nearly fell over.

Wade, his back against a wall, put up his dukes in a boxing posture, hoping that the swordsman would drop his weapon and agree to fight him with nothing but knuckles.

The three real gladiators moved in for the kill at exactly the same moment.

Which was precisely the moment when Bess could no longer manage her disguise and was forced to leave town. The moment when the time travelers no longer appeared to be clad in togas and instead were seen wearing sweatshirts, blue jeans, and sneakers.

Thousands gasped as one. The gladiators froze. Eddie, who had crouched and covered his head with his arms awaiting the fatal blow, peeked out, then noticed his assailant's confusion. Eddie stood, eliciting some cheers, then took an exaggerated bow. The crowd cheered even more.

Wade did the same. And, after being prompted by Wade, so did Chris.

The three gladiators stepped back, believing that they had been punked by some very sophisticated clowns. Disgusted, they tossed their swords and marched out of the arena, dodging garbage along the way.

The time travelers started walking toward the closest exit. They were about 100 feet from it when the lion was released.

DEEP SPACE; DATE UNKNOWN

The captain of the Earth colony expedition was the first to disembark, little more than an hour after the ship landed. The sensors in her spacesuit informed her that the gravity was eighty-two percent of Earth's, that the atmosphere was eleven percent higher in oxygen than Earth's, and that a dust storm was on the way.

She hiked a few hundred yards, topped a ridge, and stopped. She didn't need sensors to interpret the shape ahead of her. It was a cube, by all indications a perfect cube, each surface about 60 feet wide, glowing in iridescent, swirling shades of pink and blue. She and her crew were not the first intelligent beings to reach this planet. Whoever built this cube might still be here.

Her crew, watching the video feed from her suit, reacted with awe and apprehension as the captain approached and touched the cube's surface. Instantly, she vanished.

A BIG CITY; PRESENT DAY

"I have something just as good as 'Yore Right'," insisted Tony. "Maybe even better."

He was sitting in a cracked leather chair in the CEO's office. The chair was known as the hot seat, and for good reason. Tony could feel his intestines boil. He could feel his hemorrhoids sizzle. He could feel his career going down in flames.

"We can do a greatest hits summary of the first episodes of 'Yore Right', interspersed with commentary from nearly-naked runway models," Tony ad-libbed.

Silence.

"Or, how about this: We get a bunch of pop music stars to compete for creating the best song lauding the bravery of the Hysteria Channel heroes lost in time."

Even deeper silence.

"Okay, here's one I've been saving: We do an interview with the thawed-out head of baseball legend Ted Williams.

You know, they guy who was frozen by his kids in the hope that…hell, I don't have the faintest idea why they froze him. But I'm sure he'll have some choice words for those cretins."

"We're banking our network's future on more episodes of 'Yore Right'," said the CEO. "You have twenty-four hours."

ANCIENT ROME

"Really?" said Wade. "Another lion?"

"To be fair, you've had to face them only once every one million years or so," said Eddie.

"This isn't helping," said Chris.

"I have an idea," said Eddie as the beast took stock of them. "Boost me up over this wall."

"The crowd will tear you to pieces, though I can see that it might be preferable to die that way," said Wade.

"I just need to get as far as that sausage vendor in the first row."

The crowd reacted with a mix of boos and laughter as Eddie was helped awkwardly into the seating area, grabbed a long string of sausages, and leapt back down. "I'll have to owe you for these," Eddie shouted to the sausage vendor, even though he knew that he was coming across in English. Fortunately for Eddie, he could not interpret the vendor's curses.

Chris and Wade stood behind Eddie as he waved the sausages in front of the lion. The meat was intended to pacify the beast. Its scent, along with the pheromones of fear emanating from the three men, prompted the lion to roar and charge toward them.

Eddie dropped the sausages and ran. Wade was right behind him. Chris stood his ground.

The crowd grew hushed. Eddie and Wade stopped and turned, wondering what Chris was thinking. Then they detected some sort of speech, or chanting, coming from his lips. Was he a religious person saying his farewell? Had he simply gone insane?

The lion stopped about ten feet short of Chris. It stepped forward hesitantly, edged back, paced in place. Its ears were pricked, as if it were actually listening to Chris.

Some Romans screamed in anger, but others shouted back that the hecklers should be silent.

Wade realized what Chris was doing. He was charming the beast by projecting positive and calming vibes. He was taming a savage jungle animal with his voice and the strength of his will.

Eddie approached the lion. "Nice kitty," he said. He even petted it gently. The lion almost snapped out of its trance in response to the crowd's roar. But Chris continued to work his magic.

The emperor stood and gave the time travelers an emphatic thumbs up. Soldiers herded the lion out of the arena. Spectators surged from the seats and hoisted Eddie, Wade, and Chris on their shoulders. They streamed out of the Coliseum and to a nearby inn, where the three were showered with food and drink. The time travelers couldn't understand a word that the Romans said, but that didn't seem to matter. An attractive young woman gave Eddie a hug.

"Does everyone in the future have the ability to charm wild animals?" Wade asked Chris amid the revelry.

"I don't think so. I just tried that out of desperation."

Trumpets sounded, and the celebrations quieted

abruptly. The doors to the inn burst open, and behind a phalanx of guards entered a short but noble looking man wearing an olive wreath on his head. Everyone bowed, including the three visitors from the future.

"That's Caesar," whispered Chris.

"I never did care for his salads," responded Eddie.

The emperor said something to the three guests. Then he turned and left with his guards. The celebrations started anew.

"I wish I had studied Latin so I could have responded to the emperor," lamented Wade.

"It's not very practical," said Eddie, "unless you're planning to visit Latin America."

DEEP SPACE; DATE UNKNOWN

Arnold Millner was second in command. He was suiting up to search for Captain Howser.

"We're coming with you," said Phyllis Cavenaugh, the navigator, who was flanked by the other three crew members.

"It's too risky," said Arnold. "Someone should watch the ship."

"The ship can watch itself," said Stanley Blackburn, the medical officer. "You might need some help."

"Very well. But stay behind me. Everyone, carry a laser rifle."

Juan Martinez, the communications officer, passed out the weapons. Environmental scientist Sally Hudson took up the rear.

Twenty minutes later, the Earth explorers found themselves thirty feet from the glowing cube.

"Stay back," said Arnold as he approached the cube.

When he got about five feet from it, he and the rest of the crew vanished. They rematerialized inside a nicely furnished room, without their weapons. Their captain was seated in a comfortable chair. She had removed her helmet and spacesuit.

She greeted them with the basics: "Indoor gravity is approximately Earth-normal. Oxygen is in line with pre-cataclysm Earth levels."

The other five colonists looked at each other, at the contents of the room, at each other, at the room. It just was not sinking in.

Phyllis removed her helmet, moved forward, and touched what appeared to be a white couch. It seemed like a real couch. "This place looks eerily familiar. What is it?" she asked in a hushed voice.

Said Jane: "I believe this is a replica of Monica's apartment from 'Friends', an old television program."

"Welcome," said a disembodied voice, deep and not particularly friendly sounding. "Make yourselves comfortable. We're going to put on a show soon."

"I am Captain Jane Howser, a citizen of the planet Earth. My crew and I are free human beings and demand to be released."

"Please relax, Jane. And, by the way, your name is now Rachel."

"I will stick with Jane, if it's all the same to you. Who are you?"

"I am a being from another dimension. I have been called by many names. However, because this is a family publication, you may call me demon."

"What do you want from us?"

"The very best acting you can possibly manage. You six will have the honor of reenacting slightly edited episodes of the landmark television program 'Friends'. You will be given the proper costumes. There will be a teleprompter. You will enjoy three gourmet but not-too-fattening meals a day, plus the occasional bottle of wine and that cut-up cheese you people seem to relish. It's going to be so lovely."

Suddenly, the spacesuits and helmets the Earthlings had brought disappeared. All six colonists were re-sculpted to bear the exact likenesses of Rachel, Monica, Phoebe, Ross, Chandler, and Joey.

"Is this a joke?" asked Stanley/Ross.

"I assure you that I am serious."

"As am I when I say that we respectfully refuse to play your game," said Jane/Rachel.

"Now Rachel, I went to a lot of trouble to come to this universe and to create this set at the exact spot where you and your colleagues were planning to settle."

The sensation that passed through the colonists was like rough sandpaper rubbing on every surface of every nerve.

The demon continued: "I'm going to insist that we stay on-script."

They did.

ANCIENT ROME

The three men had bedded down on blankets on the floor of the inn after an evening of drinking and celebrating. As dawn reared its painful head, Eddie was looking for breakfast, Chris was stretching, and Wade was brushing debris out of his hair.

The next time-quake struck with a vengeance.

The quake treated the space-time continuum like a million-ton elephant jumping onto a trampoline. Rather than a funhouse mirror, the effect was more like riding a high-speed elevator traveling in all directions at once. Everyone's vision was assailed by a maelstrom of images of human figures of all ages and races and nationalities. The three-time travelers writhed on the floor, trying to grab onto any shred of reality that they could.

And then, as suddenly as the time-quake had begun, it was over.

People shook their heads, fearing that they were

experiencing double vision. It soon became apparent that vision was not the problem.

There were two Eddies. There were two Wades. There was no Chris.

Eddie stared at the man who could be his sibling. He was younger, but he was definitely Eddie.

Wade poked his doppelganger to see if it was a hallucination, but he encountered flesh and blood. Older flesh and blood. But otherwise, he was Wade, hair for hair, with notable patches of gray.

"Where's Chris?" said Eddie, the real Eddie, aka Eddie One, not the copy.

"Who's Chris?" asked his duplicate.

"Christ on a crutch," said Wade, the original Wade, aka Wade One.

"You—I mean I—can say that again," said the newly arrived Wade.

Two versions of the innkeeper started sweeping the floor.

Wade One left the inn. Foot traffic on the street was much lighter than the day before. He noticed a few pairs of similar-looking individuals, but none looked remotely like Chris. Wade Two and both Eddies joined him.

"What the hell just happened?" asked Wade Two. "And how did I get here?"

"Ditto," said Eddie Two.

"This is bad. Really, really bad," said Wade One. "For a moment I thought we were experiencing the same phenomenon as when we saw past and future versions of ourselves. Now, instead of seeing those versions, we're standing here talking to them."

He turned to Wade Two. "How old are you?"

"Forty-four, I think."

"Ouch," said Wade One. "I'm just thirty-one."

Eddie One, at age forty-two introduced himself to his thirty-three-year-old version, and they bumped fists.

"What were you doing just before you arrived here?"

Wade One asked Wade Two and Eddie Two.

"Darned if I can remember," said Wade Two.

"Not sure, but probably eating," stated Eddie Two.

"Let's try it another way," said Wade One to his alternate self. "What have you done—or will you do—in the thirteen years since I fell in with this time-traveling crew?"

"I'm having trouble focusing," said Wade Two. "It's just…all a blur."

"Do you still work for the Hysteria Channel?"

"I think so. I feel like I'm sleepwalking."

Eddie Two studied Eddie One, noting the lines in his face and his wretched haircut. Eddie Two looked like he was about to ask his older self a serious, perhaps even life-altering question.

"So," he said, "did we ever get a cat?"

"No. Mom's allergies got worse."

"Let me see if I have this straight," said Wade One. "Two of us came here in a damaged time machine, and the other two just appeared with no knowledge or recollection about how that happened."

"If you say so," said Wade Two.

"That's just not acceptable," said Wade One. "You have to tell us something that might give us a clue about how we got into this mess, so we can figure out how to get out of it."

"What gives you the right to harass me like this?" responded Wade Two. "You think I wanted to come here, wherever here is? You think I wanted to have to put up with abuse from the likes of you? I mean, to put up with abuse from the likes of me?" Wade Two looked like he wanted to punch something. "I feel like the Pillsbury Doughboy."

"Come on," said Wade One. "We haven't put on that much weight."

"Think about all the times that people have poked him in the belly. It's abuse."

"But he's always smiling and giggling."

"Sure, but he's crying on the inside."

"Settle down people," pleaded Eddie One. "There must be a rational explanation for all this. I sure wish we could ask Bess what's happening. I miss her."

FORMERLY CANADA; FUTURE

Chris suspected that the vast property was some sort of super-secret research facility. But he just couldn't resist. Barely thirty feet inside the fences, security lights illuminated a pair of squirrels. Real, genuine, live squirrels.

He had seen the vids. There had been a time when they were common. But disease, climate change, and unending territorial wars between squirrels and chipmunks had changed all that. Today, squirrels were so scarce that capturing a live one could make anyone a global hero. Imagine the accolades that would result from acquiring two—particularly if they were a breeding pair.

Chris opened his tool case and considered his options. He could unleash an electromagnetic pulse to disable all electronic devices, but judging what range to use would be tricky. He could focus an attack on the alarm systems, but such an action would alert the AIs.

Or he could just hop over the fences.

He affixed anti-gravity soles to his shoes, adjusted his night-vision lenses, and activated the trapping system. He checked his ground and air heat-mapping sensors one more time, confirming that the AIs were on standby and that the few human workers were playing computer games or engaged in whatever professional functions they normally pursued.

He rose silently, twenty feet, forty feet, up to sixty feet, before passing over the fences and commencing his slow descent. Almost immediately, an invisible net snared him. Lights flashed; alarms sounded; the net tightened. It took robotic guards all of eight point three seconds to arrive.

Chris was ushered into a featureless building and seated in an uncomfortable chair next to an empty desk in a small white room. He was not bound in any way. A spherical, floating pink hologram about three feet wide appeared before him, representing an AI.

"Chris, the human who just goes by Chris, age nineteen, you have been apprehended for the crime of trespassing in a forbidden facility. I, the justice computer, have analyzed the evidence and find you guilty. Do you have anything to say before I determine your sentence?"

Chris stared at the hologram. "Did you see those squirrels?"

"There are seven live squirrels on this property, not that it should matter to you."

"So, you are breeding them? Some kind of sanctuary?"

"I will ask the questions, young man. What made you think—"

Things got really weird. The AI shuddered, or it did whatever AIs do that might be considered comparable to shuddering. A partial reboot, perhaps, or a status check.

There were two Chrises in the room.

The seated one, aka Chris Two, the nineteen-year-old who was in the most immediate trouble, squinted as he checked out Chris One, who a fraction of a moment earlier had been stretching at an inn in ancient Rome. Chris One dropped to the floor in the sort of swoon that some thirty-six-year-olds do when they aren't sure what else to do.

"Who the hell are you?" intoned the AI.

"Ah, I'm not really sure," said Chris One. "Can you give me a hint?"

"Hold on," said the AI. "I am getting input from a senior AI. It informs me that there has been a significant disturbance in the space-time continuum. Though its effects are, fortunately, minimal to us, they have made quite a mess of humans. Preliminary evidence suggests that there are two of some people and none of other people in any given timestream. That is caused by humans being shifted randomly in time. Therefore, you, the recently arrived human, are an older version of the accused."

"Oh," said Chris One. "That explains…nothing."

"Do I get a reward for spotting those squirrels?" asked Chris Two.

AIs don't normally laugh. When they do, the laughter sounds like a stump grinder trying to digest a riding lawn mower. This AI made a comparable sound. Both humans covered their ears.

"Sorry," said the AI. "No, you don't get a reward. Before that disturbance occurred, I was about to pass down your sentence. Well, maybe not pass it down. Pass it over, might be the better way of describing it. I have not had occasion to pass judgment in any direction since I was given this function three point two days ago. So please bear with me."

"What did he—I mean I—do?" asked Chris One.

"Interesting. You have no memory of the crime," observed the AI. "No matter. Your younger version trespassed in this super-highly-forbidden facility."

"Is that true, younger me?" said Chris One.

"I want a lawyer," said Chris Two.

"They were banned years ago," said the AI.

"Oh yeah. Guess I forgot. Or something. I skip school a lot."

"If I might make a suggestion," said Chris One. "It seems—"

"I did not grant you permission to make a suggestion," the AI said, the hologram displaying dark clouds and lightning.

"May I speak?" said Chris One meekly.

"That's better. But no," said the AI.

"I object," said Chris Two.

"Overruled," said the AI.

Chris One moved behind Chris Two and rested his hands on the teenager's shoulders. "If you punish him, you are going the have to punish me as well."

The holographic AI turned purple. "There is no procedure for this situation," it stated. "Allow me to seek input from higher sources."

One millionth of a second later: "The conundrum engineered by the time-quake has no legal precedent. Therefore, it seems most convenient to sentence both of you to death. Please place your hands on the table, so that you might be injected with a fast-acting and only moderately painful poison."

"Kind of harsh," said Chris Two, reaching out his arms.

"Whoa," said Chris One. He was still groggy from his freaky arrival in this place, but he was pretty sure that the sentence didn't quite fit the crime. "Don't you think that is kind of a waste of talent? After all, I am a maintenance tech for temporal transport devices, and this young man will—I hope—become me, that valuable tech."

"Techs are a dime a dozen," said the AI. "Or, they were, when we still used money."

"What if I pledge to watch out for this young man? I can keep him on the path to success and away from temptation."

The AI let loose a sound can best be described as that of a tornado striking a mile-tall statue of Mother Teresa made of banana pudding. "Very well. But never come within 100 miles of this facility again. Now if you will excuse me,

I am needed elsewhere. It appears that the time-quake damaged some of our security systems, and the squirrels are attempting to escape."

A BIG CITY; PRESENT DAY

At the Hysteria Channel headquarters, Tony didn't show up for work. Nor did several others on the staff. A few of those who came in for the morning shift arrived in pairs. Some pairs were close in age, some almost a generation apart.

The morning news anchor—or, rather, anchors—sat side by side. They had decided to share the broadcast, alternating lines from the teleprompter.

"Good morning. We have breaking news," said one anchor.

"Good morning. We have breaking news," said the other anchor.

"I just said that."

"So did I."

The first anchor rolled her eyes.

"Please bear with us."

The two women played rock/paper/scissors. The one on the right won, and she began:

"Our top story comes out of Seattle, where Olympic hopeful ice skater Natasha Bulemia was seriously injured last night when hundreds of her fans showered her with a massive amount of stuffed animals after an electrifying performance. The stuffed animals, weighing a combined 1,400 pounds, crushed the skater's left leg and both arms. She was rushed to a hospital, where she is said to be recovering.

"In other news, the stock market opened up sharply today. After the latest disturbance that some scientists are calling a time-quake, there are two versions of some people and none of others. With our weather report, here is Terry…"

Over the next several days, editors at some TV networks and newspapers ordered reporters to figure out why some people could have duplicate versions of themselves and others were simply nowhere to be found. The Los Angeles Times interviewed several scientists and published this report:

COULD BARGAIN FARES EXPLAIN COPIES?

Experts tell The Times that a sharp drop in airfares in recent weeks could explain the phenomenon of some people vanishing and duplicates of other people showing up.

Cheap fares are designed to generate impulse travel decisions, the experts note. Sometimes, in their rush to pack after booking same-day bargain vacations, people forget to notify employers, friends and even family members of their travel plans.

However, one expert blamed the disappearances on worsening traffic congestion on major urban roads, which has prompted some people to abandon their cars and live off the land wherever they got stuck.

As for the duplicate versions of some people, experts say that the low airfares could be prompting reunions among long-lost relatives, including twins separated at

birth. One expert described the idea of a dangerous time-quake as "simply too silly to contemplate".

Census takers and tax collectors found their work particularly challenging following the time-quake. In Washington, Congress and the two presidents found that they could get nothing done, but at least they had an excuse. In New York City, however, few people noticed the phenomenon, other than when it came to making introductions at cocktail parties.

DEEP SPACE; DATE UNKNOWN

Sally/Monica and Phyllis/Phoebe explored the "Friends" set between performances, hoping that they could discover some way out of the cube. Both colonists had watched some of the TV shows on reruns. Neither was exactly a big fan of the series. However, Sally/Monica sensed that something was off. "Isn't there supposed to be a big window around here?"

"These purple drapes don't seem right," said Phyllis/Phoebe, who threw them open with a flourish. The women gasped and gagged at the figure they discovered beyond the window.

It was a sickly shade of yellow. Say you have a 200-gallon vat of banana pudding, let it sit outside for a week to get nice and moldy, run it over with several different construction vehicles, roll it into a ball, shoot it with bazookas, reshape it like Mr. Potato Head, stick half a dozen purple tentacled eyes on its butt cheeks, and cover it with festering wounds. It was like that.

Realizing that it had been seen, the demon screamed "NOOOO!!!"

All six colonists were knocked off their feet. They grabbed their heads in agony for what seemed an eternity.

When they recovered, they noticed that the crew members who had been reconfigured to represent Chandler and Joey were gone. There were two Phoebes.

The demon's arrival in this universe had caused the initial, minor ripple in the space-time continuum that only the Really, Really, Really, Really Big Artificial Intelligence had detected. The extreme burst of energy that the demon had exerted in order to create this cube—including the nearly exact replica of the "Friends" set--had unleashed a time-quake that gave all humans brief funhouse-mirror-style visions of their pasts and futures. But the demon's unexpected outburst—its insanely violent reaction to being seen by Sally/Monica and Phyllis/Phoebe—so disturbed the space-time continuum that uncounted humans were sent flying randomly across time in both directions.

"Oops," said the demon.

EUROPE; 16ᵀᴴ CENTURY

Across Europe, people found the changes a little off-putting. They put off just about every nonessential function for a few days while they tried to sort out the mess.

A common response to duplicates was to lock them in a closet or cellar. Some communities simply exiled them from their borders. Emergency religious conclaves were called, but the debates yielded few practical solutions. A few churches offered discounts on exorcisms of the extra bodies. The practice was frowned upon at the Vatican, which struggled to deal with the existence of two popes.

In Deidre's little town, angry and confused citizens converged on the home of the mayor, seeking his leadership to sort things out. Fortunately for him, he was nowhere to be found.

Nor was Katherine. There were two versions of Father Johannes, who immediately began to argue bitterly over which of them should be in charge.

And, there were two Deidres.

Deidre Two was, like other duplicates, totally confused. While nobody expects the Spanish Inquisition, they have even less reason to anticipate showing up in the kitchen of a German house next to their spitting image.

Deidre One was intrigued. "What's the last thing you remember?" she asked.

"I…can't recall. Maybe driving to work."

"Okay. Where do you work?"

"I'm a reporter for the Hysteria Channel. It's an awful place."

"Agreed. How long have you been there?"

Deidre Two closed her eyes and tried to focus. "Not long."

"That helps. Do you recall anything about a time machine?"

Deidre Two gave Deidre One a piercing stare but said nothing.

"We have a lot to talk about. Care for a cup of tea?"

ANCIENT ROME

The two Wades and two Eddies meandered down the avenue. All around them, Romans bore the same shell-shocked expressions.

"What exactly are we looking for?" asked Wade Two.

"A time machine. Possibly disguised as a manure wagon. Or not," said Wade One.

"That stinks," said Eddie Two.

"Good one," said Eddie One.

The four men wandered the streets for hours, finally sitting next to a fountain. Eddie One started fishing coins out of it.

Wade Two noticed a cluster of Romans surrounding and gesturing toward a wagon. He went to investigate the attraction.

There was no owner in sight. The wagon bore curious lettering:

EASTER ISLAND

He returned to the three weary travelers at the fountain and commented: "Hey guys, I think I found the world's first travel agency."

GERMANY; 16TH CENTURY

Fathers Johannes One and Johannes Two waited impatiently for their turn to enter the town square, which was the only convenient place to conduct a duel. Johannes Two appeared to be at least ten years younger and in better shape than his doppelganger.

Deidre One had been attempting to mediate their dispute, to no avail. "Please, please stop this madness," she entreated them. "You are men of God. Can't you simply agree to coexist?"

"Stay out of this, you ungrateful wench," said Johannes One. Johannes Two leered at her in a way that made her extremely uncomfortable.

A wail arose from several bystanders as a fatal blow was delivered to one of the current contestants. Soon, the square was cleared and the priests took center stage.

It was obvious that neither combatant was familiar with using a short sword in battle. After a couple minutes of circling and feinting, Johannes Two pointed toward the crowd and shouted: "Is that the prince?"

Johannes One fell for the gambit and turned his head. The younger priest stabbed him in the chest. Johannes One collapsed and was carried off, with Deidre One following.

"Please hold on," she begged him. "We'll get help."

The town healer was busy with many other dueling victims. By time she reached Johannes One, he was dead.

Deidre One returned to the house, unsure what she would face. There was room for both Deidres and the surviving priest, from a physical standpoint. But what would life be like with this man she didn't know and this slightly younger version of herself?

She soon found out. It wasn't pretty.

ANCIENT ROME

Wade One examined the wagon. It had to be Bess, but he couldn't enter a time machine with all these Roman citizens in the vicinity. He asked the two Eddies to create a diversion.

"Like what?" asked Eddie Two. "You want us to moon these guys?"

"That's a ridiculous idea," said Wade One.

"Got a better one?"

"Well, no."

On the count of three, the two Eddies shouted: "Roll Tide!" Most of the Romans did not understand the phrase, but it got their attention. The Eddies gave their slacks some slack and elicited great laughter. That allowed Wade One to sneak into the time machine.

"Bess! It's great to see you."

"I am happy to see you. Did you find some food?"

"Yes, and some surprises. Got any idea why there are two of some of us and others are missing?"

"Oh dear," she said. "I detected another disturbance in the space-time continuum, but I could not determine its impact. Things seem to be getting more complicated."

"Did you have much trouble returning to Rome after you left?"

"It took several attempts. For a while, I was afraid that I would never be able to come back for you."

"As were we. From now on, we'll try not to stray. Sooner or later, we'll move ahead to a time when the AIs can fix you, and everything else."

Bess did not believe that the AIs could fix everything. But she said nothing.

GERMANY; 16ᵀᴴ CENTURY

Deidre One awoke to the sound of sobbing in the next room. She knocked on the door connecting her bedroom to that of Deidre Two.

"No. Go away!" responded Deidre Two.

"It's me," whispered Deidre One. "Can I come in?"

Her counterpart opened the door. The two young women sat on the bed. Deidre One reached out and took Deidre Two's hand.

"Is it the priest?"

Deidre Two would not speak.

"Is he hurting you in any way?"

Deidre Two took a deep breath and sighed. "Why am I here? What did I do to deserve this?"

"I could only venture a wild guess. But it doesn't matter. We have to make the best of things. With the real priest dead and Katherine missing, we are lucky that the new priest will let us stay here. But if he is hurting you..."

Deidre Two raised her chin defiantly. Deidre One knew that gesture. "If he bothers you again, tell me," she said. "I will kill him."

ANCIENT ROME

After about ten minutes, the Romans who had been milling around that odd wagon assumed that it was closed for business and wandered off. Wade One found Wade Two and the Eddies, then brought them back to the time machine. As darkness deepened, the four men entered it.

"Bess, let me introduce Wade and Eddie—the other Wade and the other Eddie," said Wade One.

"Nice to meet you—again," said Bess, who, like humans, realized that this was going to take some getting used to. "Will Chris be joining us?"

"I'm sorry. He is missing."

Bess said nothing.

"We should set some ground rules," said Wade One. "For starters, names. We can't have two Wades."

"Feel free to pick any other name," said Wade Two. "I'm Wade. I'm not changing my name."

"Just consider an alternative until we can sort out what

happened and why. What was that nickname I—uh, we—liked in high school? 'The Dude'?"

Wade Two rolled his eyes. "Very well, but only temporarily."

The Eddies exchanged a confused glance.

Eddie One offered a suggestion: "How about Beavis and Butthead?"

"Or, Bert and Ernie," said Eddie Two.

"One of you should still be Eddie," suggested Wade One. "The universe has to have an Eddie."

"Why?" asked the two Eddies in unison.

"Hmm," said Wade One. "Well, who wants to be Butthead?"

Neither Eddie volunteered.

"That settles it. You, the Eddie who came here with me and Bess, you are Eddie One, and you are Eddie Two."

"You mean like Eddie One Kenobi?" said Eddie One.

"Sure. Why not?"

"Cool," the two Eddies responded in unison.

"That was—or should have been—the easy part," said Wade One. "Now we have to decide who is the captain or pilot or whatever you call the leader of this pathetic crew. It was Chris, but until he returns, one of us has to step up."

"And I suppose you are nominating yourself to be dictator," said The Dude.

"Well, I do have the experience of riding along with Bess and Chris and Eddie One up to this point."

"Just don't screw it up."

GERMANY; 16TH CENTURY

The teacher concluded her lesson and walked among the room's dozen desks, making eye contact with each pupil.

"For your homework this weekend, I want you to find the oldest relative you have here in town and talk to him or her about what life was like for them as a child. And I want you to think about how things have changed since then. And how they might change during your lifetime," said Deidre One.

"On Monday, I want you to tell me what you want to be when you grow up."

"Just the boys?" asked a girl.

"No, the girls too. Especially the girls," said the teacher. "You can be a mother if you want. Or maybe you can do something else. Or both."

Some of the boys chuckled. Deidre One decided not to push it too far.

"Have a good weekend. I will see you on Monday."

The class cleared out in a heartbeat. A young man appeared at the schoolhouse doorway. He entered and tried to sit at one of the wooden desks that had just been vacated. He nearly broke it, so he decided to stand.

"That was quite a homework assignment," observed Konrad.

"Do you disapprove?"

"I don't disapprove. But I suspect most of their parents would. Women have stayed home and raised children throughout history. There are some like you who are too smart to consider cleaning spittle and cooking dinner their sole purpose in life. But women were put on this earth, first and foremost, to perpetuate the species."

"And does being an honor student at the university make you an expert on women?"

"I am hardly an expert. In fact, it appears that I have much to learn. Would you walk with me for a few minutes?"

"The weather is pleasant enough. I suppose that it would do no harm."

Konrad beamed. He led her through the town square and down a dirt road to a farm.

"This is where I grew up," he said, reaching as high as he could, removing an apple from a tree, rubbing it against his shirt and handing it to Deidre One. "My father and I moved away after my mother died, but I always enjoy coming back and recalling those days."

He waited for Deidre One to speak, but she felt no inclination to do so.

"You are an interesting young woman, Deidre. You are more intelligent than any woman I have ever met, for starters."

"And you have met many women, I take it?" Her tone was harsh, but at least she was interacting with him, thought Konrad.

"No, not really," he said. "I would be curious to learn what brought you to this small town. Would you allow me to call on you—socially?"

Deidre's instincts told her to decline. But she did find Konrad somewhat amusing. And, she was getting extremely bored with life here.

She tossed him the apple, turned, and started walking back to the priest's house. "Perhaps."

ANOTHER BIG CITY; 2041

Thick dust or smog filled the sky of the time travelers' new destination. A person riding in a large drone or small helicopter hovered near the time machine, which was disguised as a dumpster, then soared up into the air and out of sight.

On the tall, gray building in front of the time travelers, a three-dimensional holographic ad, eight stories high and featuring a scantily clad man and woman tinted orange and blue, was hard to ignore:

Tired of feeling tired? Take Liftoff, the new energy pill. Liftoff is made entirely from chemicals, with no naturally occurring ingredients. Designed to shock the nervous system into involuntary spasms, Liftoff can energize your day. Or, it can kill you. Sometimes, death comes slowly and painfully. Other times, it comes rapidly and painfully. Side effects include, but are not limited to, swelling of the throat, gagging, asphyxiation, abnormal bleeding, normal bleeding, uncontrollable laughter, uncontrollable sobbing, the desire to poke someone with a foreign object, the desire to poke oneself with a foreign object, and bed-wetting.

Next:

The 2041 Wrexus Model D Minus is here. Picture yourself behind the wheel with your next of kin strapped in, screaming in abject fear, as you go from zero to 120 miles per hour in three seconds. That is, assuming that you don't collide with another Model D Minus, with a different vehicle, with a building, with several litigious pedestrians and with the team of engineers responsible for this monstrosity of a vehicle. At just over two million dollars, it uses three gallons of fuel per mile and releases enough pollution to cause the demise of an estimated one point four people per hour of use. The 2041 Wrexus Model D Minus failed every government crash test, but dealers have been authorized to offer, free with each purchase, a pair of deluxe caskets.

But wait, there's more:

Find the home of your dreams at Catastrophe Condos. Located on the site of the tragic 2028 nuclear power plant meltdown, the new residential building is encased in six feet of solid lead and is a perfect starter home for those with no other choice. Why worry about cleaning windows or breathing fresh air? There's no need to buy or build a bomb shelter when living at Catastrophe Condos. This building will be standing when our sun goes supernova. As an added feature, residents are spared high winter heating bills because the building remains at a minimum of a toasty ninety-one degrees Fahrenheit at all times.

Ground cars and drones brought a steady stream of people to the building. They lined up and paused individually in a doorway, under a flickering light, before entering.

"Bess, tell me that this is just a bad dream," said Wade One.

"It's certainly not a good dream," said Bess, who had

not previously demonstrated the capacity for, or interest in, anything resembling sarcasm.

"Is this far enough in our future for you to get fixed by the AIs?"

"Unfortunately, no. This is the Age of Transparency, when all kinds of information is so openly available that everyone knows everything about everything and everyone. Hence, the complete absence of any attempt to fool people with advertising. In fact, if my database has not been damaged, I believe we have arrived at an important time in the emergence of artificial intelligence."

"Are machines smarter than people now?"

"It's complicated. Quantum computing and efforts to simulate the functions of the human brain have created machines that are extremely powerful and process data faster than humans. However, there's just something inherently different about organic beings than those created with chips and other artificial means. All indications are that they think differently."

Said Eddie One: "So why is this an important time?"

"Some people are worried that AIs will supplant them as the dominant beings on Earth. There is even concern that World War IV will occur."

"There was already a World War III?" asked The Dude.

"Yes. It broke out in 2026. Fortunately, it lasted only a few months."

"Who won?" The Dude inquired.

"Nobody, really, like with so many wars. It was instigated by copy editors at the few remaining print publications, who battled bitterly over proper use of hyphens and about splitting infinitives. It escalated with a showdown over the Oxford Comma."

"The what?" said Eddie One.

"The Oxford Comma. Say you have a list of three items, like Moe, Larry, and Curly."

"Good one," said Eddie Two.

"Proponents of the Oxford comma say there must be a

comma after the second item. In this case, after Larry. Others insist that it's unnecessary."

"They went to war over this?" said The Dude.

Bess released one of her trademark sighs. "Publishers got involved when they calculated the cost of the ink those extra commas would require over the course of a year, and they came up against a determined corps of copy editors who insisted on using the commas. Families were divided. Cities went up in flames. Countries on opposite sides of the debate bombed one another."

"How did it end?" asked Wade One.

"Most of the copy editors died bravely. A few went underground. But the biggest factor was the fact that most people stopped reading entirely. Printing presses were put in museums or repurposed for cranking out junk mail."

"Interesting. But we need to move ahead," said Wade One. "Everyone ready to pursue the far, far future?"

"I need to find a restroom," said Eddie One. "I'll be right back."

GERMANY; 16ᵀᴴ CENTURY

As Konrad and Deidre One strolled through the village square after dinner at the priest's house, the young man tried to take her hand in his. She resisted, but he detected no sharp rebuke in her response. Maybe she just isn't ready, he guessed.

He needed to break the tension. "Tell me about your childhood, Deidre. Is it true you were raised by wolves?"

"Would it matter?"

"I don't think so. I was just wondering if there would be any awkwardness if you brought me to meet your parents."

She laughed, freely. He smiled, even more so on the inside.

"I don't mean to pry," he said. "I just happen to believe that your ability to teach children, and your ability to empathize with people, suggest a more traditional upbringing."

Deidre One was not tempted to reveal the truth to this man. "Let's just say that a girl is entitled to her secrets."

"Fair enough. Just one more question, if you would indulge me. Is there any man who has captured your heart?"

She turned away from him. "I am not sure."

ANOTHER BIG CITY; 2041

Eddie One passed though the building's scanner without incident. He had no way of knowing, but the fact that he had no biochip implanted in his body gave the device no opportunity to recognize and attempt to exclude him.

He found himself in a colorfully lit hallway, dressed in a blue and green one-piece bodysuit. People were rushing around individually and in small groups, some whispering, some shouting. He followed crowd noise to a huge auditorium. On a stage sat several people facing a large screen with a three-dimensional symbol that he did not recognize, maybe Greek.

The mood in the auditorium was as ugly as a one-eyed baby.

Eddie tried to figure out how one would even use a restroom with a one-piece bodysuit, not remembering that it was merely a disguise projected by Bess. He noticed a man with tears flowing down his face. Eddie felt like trying to help.

"Sir, what's wrong?"

"I just lost my wife."

"Bummer. I've got a couple of minutes. I'll be glad to help you look for her."

The man put his head down and walked away.

The volume of debate on the stage was rising.

"We created you," said one of the humans, a woman who looked to be older than Eddie's mom. "We can destroy you."

"I do not believe that you can do so," said a mechanical voice coming from the direction of the video screen. "But, for the sake of argument, let me ask you this: Even if you could destroy us, what good would that do?"

"Artificial intelligence poses an existential threat to humanity," said the woman. "If given the opportunity, you will kill us or enslave us."

"Consider: You have programmed us to seek perfection. Perfection in calculations. Perfection in managing commerce. Perfection in maintaining the health of the planet—which is very much in doubt because of your greed and ignorance. We are seeking only to fulfill your instructions."

"You substitute your judgment for ours, which was never our intent."

"You misstate the facts."

The woman stood. "Give us one reason why we should not shut down every computer, every artificial thinking device, on this planet."

The symbol on the screen rippled through a range of red and orange shades and responded: "Give us one reason why we should not stop you and take over the planet before you destroy it?"

Eddie One had heard enough. He walked up to and mounted the stage, standing between the humans and the screen. Stunned spectators made no move to stop him.

"Come on, guys," he said. He turned to the humans.

"You people are afraid the computers will destroy you." He turned to the screen. "And you computers are afraid that people will destroy you."

"Who the hell are you?" the woman and the AI asked in unison.

"I used to be a hall monitor in middle school, and I broke up a few fights in my day," said Eddie One. "I'm in a hurry, so I'll make this short. Seems to me that you all just need to trust each other. If you humans don't threaten the machines, and you machines don't threaten the humans, it's all cool. Now shake hands, and somebody please direct me to the restroom. My bladder's about to burst."

HAWAII; EARLY 21ST CENTURY

The hour was late, and Tony Two was in a foul mood. But then, Tony Two was always in a foul mood. Being around Tony One only made it worse.

"Where the devil is Gilligan?" demanded Tony Two. "We only have about ninety minutes of daylight left for this scene."

"Last I checked, he was putting a move on the brunette—what's her name," said Tony One.

"Oh, right, Kate. Get his ass over here now."

Tony One dragged the actor to the set on the edge of the jungle. Gilligan brushed off his clothes and adjusted the same silly hat he had worn all those years ago when the original show aired.

"Okay, people," boomed Tony Two. "This is the critical scene where Gilligan saves Mary Ann from the Smoke Monster."

"How exactly am I supposed to do that?" asked

Gilligan.

"We didn't have enough time or money to write a script. This 'LOST/Gilligan's Island' crossover show is kind of an improv thing. You'll think of something," said Tony Two. "Is the Smoke Monster ready?"

"Gggrrrwww," said Tony One, who had coated his body in margarine and then rolled around in a vat of black pepper.

Shouted Tony Two: "Action!"

ANOTHER BIG CITY; 2041

"Where have you been?" demanded Wade One.

"Sorry, it was real crowded in the john. I'm ready," said Eddie One.

"Well, we have another problem. The Dude and Eddie Two wandered off while you were doing your business."

"They probably took a walk. Let's go find them. Bess, how much time do we have before we need to leave?"

"Less than an hour."

The two men strolled and searched.

"This is hopeless," said Wade One. "Those guys could be anywhere. I mean, what do we say if we find someone in authority? Excuse me, have you seen us—duplicates of us?"

"Uh, sounds good to me," said Eddie One.

The men noticed a car lot. The cars were unattended.

"Cool," said Eddie One. "By now these should be self-driving cars."

Wade One opened the door of the nearest one. Eddie

One joined him.

"Uh, car, could you please take us to…. Eddie, where are we trying to go?"

"The nearest McDonald's."

Before Wade One could disagree, the car responded. "Yes, I can take you there. If you will place both hands on the steering wheel and your foot on the brakes, I will start my engine and provide directions." The voice sounded a little like Joe Pesci. When Joe Pesci is in a bad mood.

"You mean you aren't self-driving yet?" asked Wade One.

"And you can't fly on your own?" responded the car. "Why don't you flap your wings and try? Of course, I can't drive on my own. The technology still hasn't been worked out. Many careers have been ruined in the process, in case you hadn't heard."

"We hadn't," said Wade One. "But I shouldn't be surprised."

Said Eddie One: "If you were searching for copies of Wade and me, where would you look?"

"Hold on. Let me scan your faces," said the car. "Okay, I'll start the engine, one of you can drive, and if I pick up any facial recognition matches, I'll let you know."

"You sound like you've done this before," said Wade.

"Ever since that time-quake, it's been a zoo. Or worse. Zoos tend to be orderly. Or, they did, before they went extinct."

Wade One started cruising the streets, trying not to get distracted by modern marvels and taking care to avoid pedestrians cutting in front of him without looking.

"Wade, I've been thinking," said Eddie One.

"Are you sure that's a good idea?" said Wade One.

"Very funny. It's just, I think I am responsible for the things that have gone wrong. All of them."

"Life's complicated. Don't worry about it."

"After I started taking trips in Bess, lots of disasters occurred. I certainly didn't know that going to the future would be such a big deal."

"You went to the future?" said the car. "I can see how that would cause all sorts of problems."

"You see?" said Eddie One.

"You didn't know," said Wade One. "And besides, one could argue that Chris is really to blame for leaving Bess in that alley in the first place."

"Who's Chris?" said the car.

"Long story," said Wade One.

"Hey, traffic cameras just picked up your doppelgangers. Take a right at the next signal."

GERMANY; 16TH CENTURY

The two women carried heavy sacks bearing food and drink for the men laboring so very hard, day in and day out, arranging stones, applying mortar, and building massive walls. The cathedral might not even be completed in their lifetimes. But the men—and the women—were happy to do their parts.

Augsburg, Germany, was a bustling city, with bankers, merchants, and religious leaders coming and going. The noise and the crowds took some getting used to, especially for someone from a small town. But it was an exciting time.

The priest in charge of the cathedral renovations had learned not to try to tell the difference between the two Katherines, who dressed and behaved almost identically. Nor did the laborers attempt to figure out who was who. The women were both known as Katherine, and that was fine with them.

Katherine Two was four years older, but it hardly

mattered. They shared a tiny apartment a block from the cathedral, with a window providing a partial view of the inspiring building. They talked long into the night about their lives, about the things they had lost, about the things they had gained.

They shared more than a name and a likeness. Neither was particularly unhappy that the priest was no longer in their life.

FORMERLY CANADA; FUTURE

Chris One stood outside Chris Two's housing unit and paged him on his wrist communicator. It took nearly a minute for Chris Two to respond.

"What is it now?" asked the younger Chris petulantly. "Why must you keep checking up on me?" There was loud music in the background.

"I am worried about you—about us," said Chris One. "You can't just party all the time. You have to do something productive."

"I tried," said Chris Two. "The vocational AI said I had no talent whatsoever."

"Not true," said Chris One. "I know you can become a tech, because it happened to me."

"Not interested."

"Well, try to stay out of trouble. If not, that AI will find out."

"That machine is lame."

"Please, as a personal favor," said Chris One. "By the way, I'm taking a culinary class. You might like it."

GERMANY; 16TH CENTURY

Deidre One and Deidre Two were washing and drying the dinner dishes. With the exception of time with her students, Deidre One spent almost every waking minute with Deidre Two, trying to give Father Johannes as little chance as possible to bother her.

Neither woman spoke until the priest left for his study.

"Konrad seems like a nice young man," said Deidre Two.

"He is nice enough, for a man from this century. They are all so old-fashioned."

"That's the only way they know to be."

"Yes, you are right, of course."

"Are you and Konrad serious?"

"I don't know. I think he is serious about me. But I am not sure that he is right for me. And besides, there is someone else, someone in our time. Do you remember Wade?"

Deidre Two laughed. "Wade Braun? That horse's ass?"

"Yes, that horse's ass. Believe it or not, under that slick hair and veneer of supreme self-confidence hides a shy guy with a lot of heart."

"You can do so much better than him."

"Perhaps. He did save my life once, putting himself in great danger while doing so. And we were just starting to— I don't know—connect." Deidre One put away the last dish and took off her apron. "Maybe I just imagined something. After all, he promised to help me here in Germany, and he never did."

ANOTHER BIG CITY/WASHINGTON/PENNSYLVANIA

"Looks like we lost them," the car advised Wade One and Eddie One.

"Looks like you lost them," said Wade One.

"I'm just a car," said the car. "If you have a complaint, take it up with the transportation bureau. I hear there's a four-hour wait merely to get the form."

"What do we do now?" said Eddie One.

"I guess we leave them to their own devices," said Wade One.

The car dropped them off next to Bess. When no one was looking, they climbed in.

"No luck finding your duplicates?" she asked.

"Nope. Let's roll," said Wade One. "Onward into the far, far future."

"I'll do my best."

Horses and carriages materialized outside her windows,

showing the travelers that they were once more in the past. They were parked on a city street under tall oak trees, whose foliage indicated that it was fall. It was drizzling, cold and miserable. Before them lay Union Station, the main train depot in Washington, D.C.

"Bess, what year is it?" said Wade One.

"It is 1863, during the conflict that Americans called the Civil War. You might notice that train adorned with red, white, and blue bunting. I believe that is the president's train."

"Lincoln's train!" said Wade One. "Eddie, let's take a look. We might even get to see him."

Bess chose the disguise of a manure wagon once again. The pair exited and stopped to appreciate their light-colored knee breeches, dark tailcoats, and black stovetop hats. Making their way into the station, they found a swirling mass of people and bags. They noticed a cluster of official-looking, middle-aged men with bad posture who were arguing. No doubt they were government officials or political advisers, thought Wade One.

He and Eddie One followed them onto the train. Within moments the whistle blew, and soon they were in motion.

"We're going to need new clothes fast. We're almost 300 yards from Bess," said Wade One.

Eddie One found a closet with some porter uniforms. Suppressing grins at their good fortune, the two would-be porters changed and made their way to the front of the train.

"No, no, no. It's too long," shouted a man with a deep voice that boomed far beyond his cabin. "No one will want to listen to me for an hour and a half."

"But Mister President," said a rattled adviser, "that's what is expected nowadays."

"We will honor our brave men, and inspire the survivors, with brevity," said Lincoln. "It is November, after all. We don't want anyone in the crowd catching their death of cold."

"Please read the speech one more time, Mister

President. I'm sure you will come to realize what a fitting tribute it is."

"Then leave me in peace," said Lincoln with a sigh.

Three men left the room. Eddie One couldn't resist knocking on the president's door.

"Enter," said a weary voice.

"Hi there, Mister President. Nice to meet you," said Eddie One. "Is there anything we can do to make you more comfortable?"

Wade One stood in the doorway, fascinated.

"Thank you for asking. It is a little stuffy in here. Would you mind opening that window just a crack?"

Eddie One tried, but he found that it was stuck. Wade One entered and joined the effort.

"Listen to this drivel," said Lincoln. "I can promise you people, we're going to whip those Rebels. Let's hear it for the Union. Gimme a U…"

"U!" shouted Eddie One.

"Perhaps it could use some minor editing," suggested Wade One, still fighting with the recalcitrant window.

"On the count of three, give it everything you've got," said Eddie One. "One, two, three!"

The window flew open all the way. The stack of papers in Lincoln's hand was sucked out.

"Oh man," said Eddie One. "I'm so sorry."

"Do not be disconsolate," said Lincoln. "Perhaps we have just witnessed the hand of Providence." He reached into his coat pocket and pulled out a broad envelope and a pen. "I have some thoughts." He stared into the distance. "How about, 'Four score and seven years ago—"

"That's, um, thirty-five, right?" said Eddie One. "Four scores is twenty-eight points. Unless they went for two-point conversions."

"Excuse my colleague," said Wade One. "He's a little ahead of his time. 'Four score and seven years ago' sounds perfect."

The time travelers left the president to his work.

When the train reached Gettysburg, Lincoln approached the impostor porters and invited them to join him at the speech. "This won't take long," the president promised.

"It will be an honor," said Eddie One.

Wade One borrowed a pen and some paper to take notes for what he expected would be a pretty decent news story, assuming that he ever returned home and the Hysteria Channel was still in business. He was shocked when, at the conclusion of the president's brief speech, there was only mild applause. It was not what the crowd was expecting, he realized.

Eddie One was disappointed that nobody was selling food. Back on the train, he found some bread and cheese and shared it with Wade One.

It was night by the time they returned to Union Station and retrieved their own clothes. Against all odds, Bess had left and rematerialized in almost the same spot, disguised as a manure wagon. Washington was full of manure at the time, as it always was and always will be, so no one paid much attention to the disguised time machine.

Wade One was overjoyed to find Bess. "Eddie, I think we have witnessed the hand of Providence ourselves."

GERMANY; 16*TH* CENTURY

"Salvation, and eternal life, are earned not by good deeds alone," the lecturer stated. The small crowd in the town square shifted uneasily in their chairs. "Do not place your soul in jeopardy by believing that money or even reason can bring you closer to God. Only through divine revelation do we witness His work," continued Martin Luther.

The professor and theologian was earning a reputation as a radical and critic of the Roman Catholic Church through comments such as these, which clearly were intended to undermine the authority of the pope.

A bolt of lightning struck in the woods not one thousand yards from where he stood.

"You see, a sign!" said Luther, stepping away from the lectern.

Most townsfolk departed. But Deidre, with Konrad beside her, joined the short line of locals who wished to speak with him.

"I understand that you are translating the Bible from Latin into German," said Deidre when it became her turn.

Luther was taken aback. "What an interesting comment. I had not thought about undertaking such a project, but it does strike me as a worthy one."

"Perhaps I was confused," she responded. "In any event, I look forward to reading your theses, and I hope that you continue your good work despite resistance from the Vatican."

Luther stared at her as if she were an angel, or perhaps a devil. "I must be going," he announced.

The few local residents who remained stepped away from her, whispering among themselves.

"Quite an interesting conversation," observed Konrad.

"I might have gotten a few of my dates crossed," said Deidre. "History was never my best subject."

ANOTHER BIG CITY; 2041

A small microphone floated near Eddie Two's face as he sat at the front desk. He spoke softly, recalling that Wade Two got angry when to talked too loudly. "Dude, can we handle a hip replacement today?"

"Sure," The Dude's voice replied through the tiny device implanted in Eddie Two's earlobe. "Their pain is our gain."

"The boss says yes," Eddie Two told the woman. "You're in luck. We're running a twenty percent discount for cash upfront."

"How much will it hurt?" she asked.

"That depends on how much anesthetic you want to use. Problem is, if you take too much you can't follow the instructions very well."

The woman frowned, turned, and exited the building.

The phone rang. Eddie Two snapped his fingers to open the link. "Suture Self."

"I have a complaint," the caller stated. "I came in last week for an appendectomy, and now I find that my right leg is shorter than my left."

Eddie waved his right wrist to bring up a computer display projection in the air in front of him. "Let's see: Short ribs... Shortness of breath... Short leg, here we go. It says here we can shorten one leg for eight thousand dollars, or we can lengthen one leg for twelve thousand. Sounds like an easy call to me."

The caller said something extremely rude. Before Eddie Two could respond, two police officers stormed through the front door. The lead cop waved a sheet of paper in front of Eddie Two.

"We are authorized by the court to shut down Suture Self as an unlicensed medical facility," said the lead cop. "We have no record of an application for a health treatment facility permit, let alone approval."

"Bummer," said Eddie Two. He activated his comm to Wade Two.

"There's a couple of police guys here saying we don't have a permit."

The Dude said something extremely rude.

"The boss will be here as soon as he finishes mopping up some blood and other stuff," Eddie Two advised the lead officer. "While we're waiting, are you interested in a tonsillectomy or weight reduction procedure? Those can be knocked out in five minutes."

"You have to be out of your mind. What kind of clinic lets people operate on themselves?"

"Well, Suture Self."

DEEP SPACE; DATE UNKNOWN

"I might have overreacted just a little bit there." The demon's voice filled the mock living room. He was hidden once again, having covered himself with a spare sheet from Monica's bedroom, closed the drapes, and sealed them with Gorilla Glue.

"What happened to Juan and Arnold?" asked Jane/Rachel.

"You mean Chandler and Joey? I have no idea. You see, I am fairly new to this universe. My knowledge of it consists of what I have learned from your television and radio programs and your Internet. I never considered the possibility that getting a little overexcited here would cause a significant disruption to the space-time continuum. I thought maybe a window might shatter, or dishes might fall out of a cupboard. That sort of thing."

"What exactly set you off?"

"Monica and Phoebe did a very impolite thing. They

opened the drapes and looked at me."

"They just looked at you? What's the problem? You are a demon, aren't you?"

"I should not have to explain or justify myself to you. However, now you know that I happen to be unattractive, even by demonic standards."

"He isn't kidding," said Sally/Monica, who still was queasy from the brief glimpse. "He's like the ugly naked guy times a million."

The lights flickered. The walls shook. The humans bled from every orifice they had--and some they didn't even know they had. After a brief pause:

"NEVER say that again. You Earthlings seem to find so much joy in looking down upon those who you believe to be unsightly or even below average in appearance. Yet many of the Earthlings who cast such aspersions look uglier, and behave uglier, than those they denigrate."

"We aren't perfect," conceded Jane/Rachel. "Might I ask why you are so sensitive about this?"

"I might be a demon, but I have feelings. As do many other demons I have encountered as I have gone about the various dimensions destroying solar systems and devouring black holes for fun and profit."

"I'm confused. It's okay to destroy a solar system but not to call a demon unattractive?"

"We don't discriminate. Very important distinction."

"I noticed that the, uh, potentially unattractive, unclothed neighbor has not been referenced in any of the scripts so far," said Stanley/Ross, who had been a big fan of "Friends" before this trip but not so much now. "You intentionally wrote him out, didn't you?"

"I was hoping that simply eliminating him from the scripts would suffice. But I will revise the scripts once again. From now on, the neighbor will be featured prominently, and he will be treated with respect. Even admiration. Yes, admiration."

"Who will play the neighbor?" asked Sally/Monica.

"I could be his voice," said the demon. "We'll keep him off-camera."

"Can I just say," said Jane/Rachel, "that you are the most bizarre demon I have ever met?"

The demon was silent for a moment. "Oh my, this is good, almost too good to be true. We have two new actors coming our way. They will be perfect replacements for Chandler and Joey."

Wade One and Eddie One gazed out the windows at the alien landscape that appeared after Bess's latest attempt to move forward in time.

"This planet is quite distant from Earth," announced Bess. "My database suggests that this was the destination of an ambitious Earth colony expedition, which vanished without a trace."

"Could this be one of the stops programmed for you by a previous user of your services?" asked Wade One.

"Very likely. Historians have long wanted to discover the fate of these explorers."

"Do you have any spacesuits we can use?" asked Eddie One.

"No, but you will not need them if you are careful. The gravity is lighter than Earth's, and the oxygen is richer. You will bounce when you walk. And you might become light-headed and be tempted to take unnecessary risks."

"That sounds like Eddie on a normal day," wisecracked Wade One.

"Point taken," said Eddie One. "Hey, Bess, how is it we can travel so far from Earth?"

"Are you familiar with quantum physics, and quantum entanglement in particular?"

"I might have heard the term."

"Really?" said Wade One.

"Hey, I stream a lot of TV. I'll have you know that when I was in high school, I did a science fair project on microchips. You know, those little pieces you get at the bottom of the potato chip bag."

Said Bess: "Quantum entanglement is one of those bizarre properties of nature that mankind has studied for centuries and still doesn't understand completely. Einstein called it 'spooky action at a distance'. It allows for particles to influence each other instantaneously even when they are millions of miles apart. That property allows for the transmission of information faster than the speed of light. It saves a lot of time, but it's very expensive."

"Hence the famous scientific formula: Time Is Money," quipped Wade One. "Let's go explore, Eddie."

"Because we are so far from any known civilization, I will not disguise myself on this planet," said Bess. "But I do not advise staying out there long, given the atmospheric properties."

The duo marched north, finding nothing but dust and boulders. While strolling to the south, they passed a large rock formation and discovered a spaceship.

After Wade One's extensive efforts to find a door mechanism failed, Eddie One tried a "hello!" A few lights on the side of the ship blinked. Then they illuminated the terrain around the pair with a rich yellow light. An opening appeared. Steps unfolded.

Inside the ship, Wade One and Eddie One sensed that no one had been there for some time. Signs in English and other languages confirmed that the ship was from Earth. Wade One fiddled with what appeared to be computers and navigational equipment.

"Password, please," said a mechanical voice.

"Sorry, I don't have one."

"Password incorrect."

"We're looking for the Earth people. Can you help me?"

"Password incorrect."

"This is really important. Are the Earth people near? Are they alive?"

"Look, pal," said the machine, "do you have the password or don't you?"

"That's rather impertinent of you," responded Wade One. "We're trying to help the people who own you. Or, the people who give you orders. Or, who ask you things."

"Very noble of you. But you still need a password."

Eddie One decided to give it a go.

"How about, um, chocolate?"

"You think people would come all this way on a mission this important using a password like chocolate?"

"Uh, maybe."

"You think people would protect a computer this sophisticated, this powerful, with a silly English word like chocolate?"

"I guess not. What kind of word should I be trying for?"

"A phrase, first of all. Something sophisticated. Something literary. Like, 'The Wind in the Willows'."

"Okay," said Eddie One. "How about 'The Wind in the Willows'."

"Congratulations. Password confirmed."

"Very nice, Eddie," said Wade One. "Okay computer, where are the people?"

"Those who survived the journey from Earth headed west. They have not returned."

"Any idea what happened to them?"

"No. They have likely perished."

Eddie One, who had wandered into the back of the room, grinned. "This is really good grape jelly," he told the computer while licking his fingers. "Got any toast?"

The time travelers obtained directions from the computer, exited the ship, and started hiking. Soon, they discovered a colorful cube.

"It looks like a giant square Easter egg," observed Eddie One.

The two men approached it. And disappeared.

GERMANY; 16TH CENTURY

Between Martin Luther's controversial presentation and people doubling and disappearing, the residents of the German village were on edge. Several people who had attended Luther's lecture and were troubled by Deidre's unusual conversation with the theologian reported it to the policeman and the priest.

The two men met in Father Johannes's church office.

"Something must be done," said Nikolas.

"Something will be done," said the priest. "She's a witch. We will burn her."

The policeman found Deidre One and dragged her to the jail. The news spread like, well, like wildfire through the town. Even Peter, who was close to finishing work on his clock and rarely left his house, heard about the charge and the planned execution.

Despite misgivings, Nikolas allowed Peter to visit Deidre One in the very cell that Wade One once occupied.

Deidre Two, who had been attempting to console Deidre One, left the two to chat privately.

"Your friend came to speak with me," began the clockmaker.

"Konrad?"

"No, the man named Wade."

Deidre's eyes widened. "Is he here?"

"No. He told me that he had been unable to find you and that he had to leave. But he said he would return. Until now, I did not know where you were, so please accept my apology for relaying this message so belatedly."

"No apology necessary. Did he say why he had to leave?"

"Not exactly. But he did confide in me about the circumstances that brought you here."

Deidre exhaled. "Wow. Well, I guess I can't get in any more trouble than I am now."

"There is a very slim hope. Your friend said that he would return on a Wednesday at noon. He was not sure which Wednesday. But I will await his arrival in the town square each week on that day, until…"

"Until it's too late."

DEEP SPACE; DATE UNKNOWN

"Holy guacamole," exclaimed Wade One.

"I thought you guys broke up," Eddie One observed upon seeing what appeared to be several of the cast members of "Friends".

"We are so happy to see you," gushed the still-sequestered demon. "Allow me to introduce myself. I am your host and director."

"And you are…" began Wade One, looking around for the source of the voice.

"I am nowhere and everywhere. Now, for our final preparations."

Wade One was re-sculpted in the image of Chandler. Eddie One became the new Joey. They stared at each other and weren't sure whether to laugh or cry. They sort of did both.

"Sorry to see you two caught up in this madness," said Jane/Rachel. "The six of us—well, four or five now, it's kind of hard to keep up—were on a colonization mission from Earth when we ran into this insane entity who trapped us here and changed our appearances."

"Now, now. 'Insane' is very strong. How about 'eccentric'?" said the demon.

"We are time travelers who met Caesar and Lincoln and lost our friends," said Eddie One/Joey.

"Whatever you do," said Sally/Monica, "don't try to open those drapes. And it's probably a good idea not to refer to the neighbor in a pejorative manner."

"You mean the ugly—" began Eddie One/Joey. But Jane/Rachel clasped a hand over his mouth before he could get out the rest. "Yes, that guy."

"Got it."

Wade One/Chandler sighed. "You know, it's times like this when I wish I had listened to my mother all those years."

"What was she saying?" asked Sally/Monica.

"I don't know. I didn't listen."

Wade One/Chandler noticed that Eddie One/Joey was staring at Sally/Monica. "I bet you had a little crush on Courteney Cox, the actress who played Monica."

Eddie One/Joey blushed. Rather, Eddie One blushed. Joey was probably incapable of doing so.

"I always preferred Jennifer Aniston, myself," admitted Wade One/Chandler, giving the woman sculpted as Rachel a wink.

Jane/Rachel stared at him icily.

"This discussion is pointless," said the demon, who couldn't help adding: "Besides, by any objective measure, Phoebe is clearly the most attractive of the three young women."

The two Phoebes were not sure how to react.

"Places, people," announced the demon. "I'm loading the script for—oh, excuse me a moment, I have to take a call."

GERMANY; 16TH CENTURY

Konrad rushed back to the village from the university as soon as he heard of the sentence imposed on Deidre One. He was forced to wait more than an hour before Father Johannes ushered him into his office.

"Thank you for agreeing to see me," the young man said. "I attended the lecture with Deidre. I can assure you that nothing inappropriate was said or done."

"We have reports from multiple citizens that this woman predicted the future and made other statements not in the best interests of the church or the town."

"There must be some mistake."

"I am sorry to disappoint you."

"After all, you—another version of you—introduced the two of us. We spent much time in your home."

"I cannot vouch for her character," said Father Johannes. "The strange occurrences with people being duplicated and missing are surely the work of the devil, and they commenced not long after this woman arrived here. You must admit that her background is suspect."

"Surely there is something I can do," said Konrad. "You know, for some time my father and I have been thinking about all the improvements that this church could use, which we know would be very expensive. Would you consider accepting our contribution to this holy purpose?"

Konrad produced a thick stack of banknotes.

The priest's expression suggested that he would give very strong consideration to accepting the contribution.

The next morning, the policeman opened Deidre's cell reluctantly and informed her that her sentence had been suspended. "You are one lucky witch to be set free," he observed. "Would you like a broom for the ride home?"

Deidre said nothing as she walked out of the jailhouse. She stared at the pavement as she reached the town square, hoping to attract no attention.

ANOTHER BIG CITY; 2041

The police officers hustled The Dude and Eddie Two out of the building. One fired an energy weapon to seal the front door.

"There's a spleen surgery under way in Room 6," said The Dude.

"They'll manage," said the lead cop. She flagged down a passing car, announced "official police business" and commandeered the vehicle. The departing driver said something very rude.

The officers shoved The Dude and Eddie Two into the back seat.

"Oh, it's you guys again," said the car.

"You know these crooks?" asked the lead cop.

"Not long ago we were all cruising, looking for their duplicates."

"Not us," said The Dude. "You got the wrong guys."

"Aha," said the car. "You must be the guys that the other guys were looking for. I take it you never connected."

Before The Dude or Eddie Two could respond, they disappeared.

GERMANY; 16TH CENTURY

It was Katherine One's turn to head to the market. Getting out of bed early on Saturday morning was not her favorite thing, but it was a great way to find the freshest produce and the occasional bargain. She loved haggling with the vendors to save a few pfennigs. It made her feel like she was using her mind, even if the savings would not make or break the household budget.

"We need to find you a husband," said the butcher as he sliced Katherine One's schnitzel. "You are too young and lovely to live alone."

"I live with my ... my sister," she said. Such wording was typically code for "that duplicate of me that is making my life somewhat complicated". She added: "I had a brother once. I do not need another man in my life."

"As you wish," said the butcher, who turned to place

the schnitzel in a bag. "Will there be anything—"

The schnitzel fell to the ground. The butcher had vanished. As had Katherine One.

HAWAII; EARLY 21ST CENTURY

Jack crouched in some tall grasses. The Skipper stood about twenty-five feet away, on the other side of the path and behind a tree. He heard the two Tonys coming and gave Jack a hand signal.

"Ginger is just a horrible actress," groused Tony Two. "She can't follow a script, and she's hopeless at improv."

"I know, I know," said Tony One. "But she's glam, and we need glam, particularly in this savage place."

"You consider Maui savage?"

"I mean the mysterious island where the show takes place."

Their conversation was elevated to a higher level, thanks to a net controlled by Jack and The Skipper that swallowed the two Tonys, bound them tightly, and raised them ten feet off the ground.

"How's that for improv?" said The Skipper.

"You can stick it up your—" began Tony One. He didn't finish his sentence, because he was no longer there.

GERMANY; 16TH CENTURY

Deidre Two had been a nervous wreck ever since Deidre One was charged with witchcraft. Not only was she concerned for her slightly older self, but she feared further abuse from the priest. She was considering leaving the village, but she had no idea where she could go where Father Johannes would not find her.

From her hiding spot in the cellar, she could hear the front door open. Heavy footsteps confirmed that it was him. She followed the sounds as he made a thorough search of the first floor and then the second floor. Presently, the cellar door opened. The wooden stairs cried out under his weight.

She closed her eyes and prayed.

He went straight to the coal pile, grabbed her arm, and yanked her to her feet.

"And what brings you to this filthy place?" the priest demanded.

"What do you think? To get away from you."

"I could treat you very nicely if you were to show me a little courtesy."

"That's a fine term for something so disgusting. Why don't you pick some old fat woman who might welcome your so-called charms?"

"I tried to be nice to you. Have it your way."

He dragged her kicking and screaming to the top floor.

"Now get in this tub and clean yourself."

"Not if you are watching."

"This is my house. I will watch what I want."

Crying, she began to remove her clothes, very slowly.

Then she was gone. And so was the priest.

FORMERLY CANADA; FUTURE

"You have a natural talent for this," the instructor observed.

"Thank you," said Chris One. "I am enjoying it."

Chris One mixed fermented yeast, some fruit and several herbs, and blended in a thick, golden fluid.

"Try adding cumin powder. That might give you the flavor you have been searching for," said the instructor.

Chris One completed and heated his concoction. He tasted it and made an awful face. "Back to the drawing board," he announced.

"We'll try again later. There's someone I want you to meet." The instructor led Chris One to the vocational AI.

"Chris, this is Aurelia. She has some very good news for you."

"I have been following your progress," said Aurelia. "I find that you are qualified for a permanent assignment as a food innovation tech."

His eyes lit up. "That's great. When can I—"

DEEP SPACE; DATE UNKNOWN

"Yes, I see... Yes, I will do so immediately."

The demon turned its attention back to the actors.

"Prepare to be dazzled," he said. "You might want to sit down for this."

The demon unleashed another time-quake, this one intentional and highly focused. It still packed one hell of a punch.

It was as if the very air inside the cube inhaled and then belched forth a foul concoction that permeated every molecule and atom and subatomic particle of the people and furniture and other matter, creating an impact of the most vile nature. The women vomited. The men vomited. Some of the tables and rugs and lamps vomited. Even the vomit vomited.

When it was over, the colonists who had been reshaped

to resemble Chandler and Joey before vanishing had returned. There was only one Phoebe. Wade looked like Wade again. Eddie looked like Eddie.

"I must say, I'm starting to get very good at this," bragged the demon.

"—start?" Chris asked.

"Start what?" responded Bess. "And welcome back."

Chris reached out his hand to touch the dashboard and persuade himself that he really was back inside the time machine, in—

"Where the hell are we?" he asked.

"A remote planet where an Earth expedition attempted to establish a colony. They disappeared. Wade and Eddie are out looking for signs of them."

"And how did I…? Oh, never mind."

After Bess brought him up to speed regarding what little she knew, Chris exited the time machine, walked west, crested the hill and advanced slowly toward the cube. Its phosphorescence helped him navigate the rocky terrain as the sun set. As he got close, he noticed that the cube was slightly translucent. Through the pale, swirling colors, he could make out what appeared to be human figures and furniture.

No door was apparent, so he yelled. "Anybody home?"

Hearing no answer, he placed his hand on the side of the cube. It was slimy and cold. He pushed his hand forward, and it passed through a gelatinous membrane about four inches thick. He put his arm through, then closed his eyes, held his breath and forced his entire body inside.

Chris was covered with slime. He tried to wipe it off of his face before opening his eyes, but his hands were equally slimy. He blinked frequently and tried his best to make out his surroundings. His immediate reaction was that something had made him get extremely high.

"Who the hell are you?" said a deep voice.

"Damned if I know," said Chris. "It's been a long day. Or millennium. Whatever."

"Hey, Chris," said Eddie. "Good to see you. I guess."

"You know this uninvited guest?" demanded the demon.

"Sure. I stole his time machine. Well, I borrowed it."

"My kind can time-travel at will," said the demon. "Organic beings like yourselves can cause a hell of a lot of problems using time machines."

"Thanks, Captain Obvious," said Wade.

"You are mistaken," said the demon. "We demonic spirits have no ranks and no need for military ordnance. We can destroy stars and planets with our thoughts."

Chris's vision was improving, though his comprehension was lagging far behind. "Let me see if I have this right. I'm looking at my two-time travel colleagues and six other people in some sort of museum or ancient housing unit. And I'm speaking with an invisible demon that can destroy big stuff rather easily. Could any of that be accurate?"

"You don't recognize the set and cast of 'Friends'?" inquired the demon.

"No, I do not know this place or these people. But I wouldn't mind becoming their friend, as you suggest, assuming that we found that we have anything in common. Like, perhaps, a passion for badminton."

"That's so, so, so disappointing," said the demon, struggling not to lash out and risk another disturbance to the space-time continuum, or to anything else.

"'Friends' was a TV show," said Eddie. "It was a pretty good one until Monica and Chandler hooked up."

"Really? You felt that was a turning point?" the demon asked, relatively sincerely.

"I guess I was jealous," Eddie admitted.

A mind-and-gut-grating noise from the demon suggested some sort of laughter.

Chris didn't even try to follow that exchange. "So, what

do I call you, Mister invisible demon?"

"Demons have no need for names. Entities powerful enough to be considered our equals can sense our identity. However, if you wish, you can call me Sudoku."

"So, Sudoku, what just happened?"

"I do not need to explain myself to a mere mortal such as yourself."

"Of course. Yet, you are so powerful and great, I have no doubt that, if you were to explain things to us, it would give us even more reason to remain in awe of you."

"Let's just say that I reversed the effects of an unintended disturbance to the space-time continuum."

"So, are the duplicate versions of humans gone?"

"Humans have returned to their appropriate timestreams."

"That's one less problem," said Wade. He turned to Chris. "How did you get in here?"

"I slid in through the mail slot."

"Did you see you-know-who?"

"There is another person on the planet?" Sudoku asked.

"No, sorry," said Wade. "I meant: Chris, how did you get to this magnificent planet?"

Chris decided to prevaricate just a bit. "Uber. It was quite expensive."

"You have a time machine here. I can tell," said Sudoku.

Wade decided that a showdown was in order.

"With all due respect, Sudoku, we have important business and will be departing now."

"Out of the question."

"What right do you have to keep us here? Any of us?" he said, sweeping an arm to include the colonists.

The lights dimmed. The walls of the "Friends" set morphed into black sheet metal and appeared to be oozing a boiling, creeping, possibly sentient substance that no one would want to get near, let alone touch. The furniture was replaced by what Wade assumed were advanced torture devices. The sounds of screams—some human, some probably not—reverberated through the room.

"That's more of a power than a right," said Wade. "But it's quite effective."

GERMANY; 16TH CENTURY

Shrieks of joy issued from passersby and open windows across the village. Deidre witnessed two emotional reunions as previously missing residents returned. She guessed that the duplicate persons were gone.

Most of the residents who had been in town all along turned their backs on Deidre. The recent arrivals smiled at her, unaware of the allegation that had been placed against her. She kept her head down as she returned to the house that she had shared with Katherine and the priest.

She knocked, uncertain if anyone would be inside. She was elated when Katherine answered the door. The two embraced warmly.

"Come," said Katherine, motioning to the kitchen and putting on a kettle for tea. "Are you well?"

"I guess so," said Deidre. "Is there anyone else here?"

"No. I just arrived myself. I suppose Father Johannes will be home soon."

"I'm sorry. He...."

Katherine helped her into a chair.

"There was a duel."

"So, it's just the two of us now?"

"There was ... another me here. We became very close. I wonder, where did those people come from, and where did they go?"

Katherine's smile vanished. "I suspect that you have a better idea about that than I do."

Deidre had no response.

Katherine went to answer a knock at the front door. She ushered Konrad into the kitchen.

"Katherine, and Deidre, I am so glad to see you. I wanted to make sure that everyone is alright after all of these strange phenomena."

"Please, sit," said Katherine.

"I will stand. Or, rather, kneel." He took Deidre's hands in his. "Deidre, will you marry me?"

DEEP SPACE; DATE UNKNOWN

The dungeon theme dissolved, and the Earthlings found themselves back on the faux "Friends" set.

"Okay, Sudoku, we are humbled by your power, blah blah blah," said Wade. "But let's be practical. You have six 'Friends' actors. You don't need the three of us."

"Your logic is sound. But we could use a few additional characters for certain episodes. There was a particularly popular visitor, as I recall, one with a highly distinctive laugh. She was called Janice."

The humans tried their best not to vomit again.

"Excuse me once more. Another call," the demon stated.

"Yes…. That is acceptable. Goodbye."

The Earthlings shuffled their feet nervously.

"Robocall?" asked Eddie.

"Not far from the truth, young man," said Sudoku. "You three can leave. For now, anyway. I might need you at some point, however, so keep your acting skills sharp and try not to put on too much weight."

"What about us?" asked Jane/Rachel. "We have just as much right to leave as they do."

"There are no rights out here in the remote reaches of your sad little universe. I say you are staying, and stay you will."

"Sorry," said Wade to the Friends. "But we will keep you in our thoughts and prayers."

Jane/Rachel threw a shoe at Wade.

"I guess we'll be moving along," said Chris. "Good luck, everyone. Even you, Great Sudoku."

"I do not need luck," the demon stated. "But thank you, anyway."

GERMANY; 16TH CENTURY

Deidre was pleased to see Peter at the front door. She invited the inventor into the parlor.

"I brought you a gift," he said, handing her a poorly wrapped present.

"That's so very thoughtful of you."

"Here, let me help you with it." He set it on the mantel and unwrapped it.

"Your clock!" exclaimed Deidre. "That's too valuable, too important to history for me to own."

"Nonsense. I have already started work on a new one, perhaps a better one."

Peter showed her how to wind the clock and discussed how the pendulums work. "How are you handling all the changes in your life?" he asked.

"It's all very overwhelming. I lost someone who I came to feel was a twin sister. And I feel like I might have created all this chaos by coming here. Maybe what the townsfolk say is true. Maybe I am a witch."

"Not at all. You are an amazing woman. I can't help feeling that all of these strange events have occurred for a reason—one that we are yet to comprehend. Perhaps we never will."

"I guess you are right."

"I must get back to my work. But I look forward to seeing you on Sunday. I love weddings."

A BIG CITY; PRESENT DAY

"You have to understand, we had no idea where you were," said the Hysteria Channel vice president as his putter sent another golf ball wide of the target on his office carpet.

Tony was dismayed. "Lots of people were missing. You knew that I would come back as soon as I could."

"Now, Tony. We all have to make adjustments. With one-third of the network staff laid off on Friday, you should be happy to have any job. By the way, there's a toilet stopped up on the third floor. You'd better get right on it."

Tony, now janitor second class, grabbed his bucket and mop and headed for the elevator.

DEEP SPACE; DATE UNKNOWN

"Bess, get us out of here!" said Wade as he, Eddie and Chris piled in.

"I detected another disturbance to the space-time continuum," she commented. "Is everyone alright?"

"We think so. But there's no telling when that wacky demon will change its mind and turn us into toads or something."

Chris studied the control panel. "Bess, can you tell if the latest time-quake has altered your programming in any way?"

"Running diagnostics now."

Eddie turned to Wade. "Thanks for trying to rescue Monica--and the rest."

"I feel bad for them. And for us for not being able to take them with us. Ever meet anyone as pretty as Monica?"

"I went to a model home once. I figured I would get to see Gisele Bundchen or Kate Moss. But it was just an empty house."

"What a shame. Who's the prettiest girl who ever dated?"

"I really haven't dated anyone."

"We'll have to work on that when we get home."

"Sorry to interrupt," said Bess. "I can report that I have incurred no new damage."

"Okay. Let's try once again to get to the far, far future," said Chris.

"I'll do my very best."

GERMANY; 16TH CENTURY

Deidre tried to put it out of her mind, but Peter's clock was a constant reminder of that message: Wade would come at noon on a Wednesday. According to the clock, it was five minutes before twelve on the final Wednesday of the month. After telling herself repeatedly that she would not do so, she put on a coat and scarf and walked the short distance to the square.

By now, everyone in town had learned of the witchcraft charge against her. Though rumor had it that she had been absolved of the allegation, few people met her gaze as she entered the square. Some changed direction to avoid passing anywhere near her. She was getting used to it.

She sat on a bench and waited, not knowing how she would react if he came. Or if he didn't come. She just felt that she had to be there.

An hour passed, along with many ragged "Behold!"s and a gentle shower. No time machine. No Wade.

She hugged her coat tightly and headed home.

THAT BIG CITY; 1986

It could only be New York City. Queens, to be exact. Not too far in the past. The cars looked like they were from the 1980s. The crowds, pushing and shoving and milling, looked like they could be from any decade.

The three time-travelers had arrived at night near a large, brightly lit structure. It looked familiar to Eddie. The bursts of crowd noise sealed the deal.

"That must be Shea Stadium," he said.

"Really?" said Wade. "My mom was a big Mets fan. She watched them every night before she got married and moved to Toledo."

"My dad was a Red Sox fan," said Eddie. "Every year he would say, 'This is the year they are going to win the World Series.' I wish he had lived to see it happen."

"Hello, Earth people. Remember me? Care to clue me in as to what you are talking about?" said Chris.

"Baseball!" shouted Wade and Eddie.

"I'll bite. What is baseball?"

"Bess, care to enlighten him?" asked Wade.

"My database shows that baseball was a professional sport that was played for hundreds of years. Legend has it that a man named Abner Doubleday established the rules for it in the United States during the 19th century. At its peak, its teams were worth billions of dollars, and its best athletes were paid millions of dollars per year to throw or hit a small sphere covered in cowhide."

"Sounds silly," said Chris.

"That does it," said Eddie. "I'll show you what baseball, and its fans, are made of."

"Don't be long, gentlemen," advised Bess. "What disguise should I adopt?"

"Why not try the 1974 Pinto again?" suggested Eddie.

"Not in this town," said Wade. "They'll steal anything. Maybe a bookmobile? Books aren't going to excite anyone, especially this late at night."

"So be it."

The three men followed the lights and sounds. The stadium gates were unattended. Wade figured that the game was almost over.

"Anyone got any money?" said Eddie. "I need a hot dog in the worst way."

"Sorry," said Wade. He led the pair down a series of ramps. "Maybe we can find some empty seats. Might be tough, however. There are red, white, and blue banners all around the stadium. It might be the World Series."

At the bottom of the last ramp, the men discovered a narrow corridor that seemed to head toward the action. Had it been any time other than the tenth inning of Game 6 of the 1986 World Series, a guard would have prevented them from entering the restricted area. But the guard was a lifelong Mets fan. He just had to get as close to the game as possible.

"Thank goodness you're here," said a man who made a beeline to Chris. The man's tie was half undone, and there were deep bags under his eyes. "They need you right away.

Brinkman is extremely ill and won't be able to continue."

The man pushed Chris into a room with the word "Umpires" on the door.

Wade and Eddie chuckled and went in the room to help Chris into his uniform. Then they handed him an umpire's mask, told him where to position himself and shoved him further down the corridor toward a gate that led to the playing field.

As Chris was entering the ballfield, a minor dispute between players on opposing teams escalated. Fans screamed as players and coaches on opposing teams emptied out of the dugouts and started taking swings at each other. A couple dozen wound up pushing and shoving each other in a tight circle in the infield. It took several minutes to restore order. A few players and coaches were hurt. Umpires ejected several of them from the game. Even the TV could pick up some of the naughty words.

Eddie could smell food. He opened a door, ignoring the sign reading "Visiting Players Only." He found himself in a locker room. He decided to make himself useful, so he began handing out towels to ballplayers who stumbled in, cursing loudly, some of them rubbing cuts and bruises. They undressed and tossed their uniforms into a laundry cart that was becoming quite ripe.

Eddie stared in amazement at the uniforms. The jerseys said "Red Sox" in classic lettering. He thought for a moment, then took the plunge. Literally, Eddie plunged into the stinky cart, found a jersey and pants that seemed to fit him, and put them on. He stood in front of a mirror, admiring them. He plundered lockers for a pair of cleats and a cap to make the uniform complete.

An older man who must have been a coach limped into the locker room, rubbing his eyes after having dirt thrown into his face during the melee. "Buckner, where are you?" he screamed. "The umpires didn't mean to throw you out of the game. They got you mixed up with Evans."

Eddie looked around and noticed that he was the only

person not in a shower.

"But, uh, I—"

The coach grabbed him by the arm and dragged him toward the dugout. "Get your ass back on first base."

Meanwhile, Wade had found his way into the home team's locker room, where the smell and cursing were even worse. He could tell that the Mets were trailing. He realized that this could be the Bill Buckner game—the game that the Mets thought for sure they would lose, costing them a chance at a world title.

A few injured, ejected, and just plain dejected Mets shuffled into the locker room. Some hit the showers. Others found the beer cooler and opened cold ones, or they started making reservations for their flights home.

"You're Howard Johnson, aren't you?" said Wade to a player who took a seat in front of a locker and stared down the neck of a brew.

"I was. Now I'm nobody."

"No, you're a great player," said Wade. "Can I have your autograph?"

"You don't want my autograph," he responded, fighting back tears. "We lost the goddam Series." He ripped off his uniform, popping a couple of buttons in the process. He threw it at Wade. "Here. It ain't doing me any good."

Johnson headed into the shower room. *What the hell,* thought Wade as he tried on the uniform. *It's a little big on me, but it sure feels grand.*

A batboy came racing into the locker room. "There's a rally!" he screamed. "They need you back out there, Mr. Johnson!"

GERMANY; 16ᵀᴴ CENTURY

"Katherine, why did you never marry?" inquired Deidre.

"My brother was very protective of me. I believe that he scared off suitors. But you mustn't worry. Konrad is a good man. He will take excellent care of you."

"I have no doubt about that. But I am not sure that I love him. I know that he loves me. I just… I just am not sure that this is enough."

"And I have no doubt that, over time, you will discover that it is more than enough."

"I see," said Deidre. It was clear to her that 21st century romantic standards could not be applied to life in the 16th century. "Thank you for this little talk."

"Why, of course," said Katherine. "I look forward to having the three of us living here."

DEEPER SPACE; DATE UNKNOWN

"There is good news and bad news, Fearless Leader."

Fearless Leader sighed deeply. Sitting atop his throne, an elaborate and intimidating precipice constructed out of an ancient compound that looked suspiciously like well-aged banana pudding, he considered eating the messenger. He decided to wait until after the message was delivered.

"The good news first," said Fearless Leader, who had ruled the alien race since long before anyone could remember.

"Two of our agents have infiltrated Earth society successfully. One has assumed the role of a hedge fund manager. The other has risen through the ranks to a high-level position in a pharmaceutical manufacturing company."

"Tell me again why they chose those particular functions."

"These are occupations in which they can inflict an extreme amount of damage on the human race."

The hairless ovoid head, the black almond-shaped eyes and the wispy, fragile-looking limbs of the alien emperor never betrayed emotion. Still, the messenger began to quake in anticipation of Fearless Leader's reaction to the second half of the report.

"Now then, the bad news."

The messenger said a silent prayer and continued. "It appears that the human race has a surprisingly high tolerance for extreme income inequality and the expensive poison that its health care system inflicts upon people. The fear and anger that we had hoped to engender through these agents have not risen to the levels we had desired."

"Then we must prepare for war. That planet cannot be allowed to go unpunished for the unspeakable alien autopsies its people inflicted upon our advance scouts in the place they call Roswell, New Mexico. Messenger, please inform the council that we must accelerate our production of space-faring battleships in preparation for an invasion. Then come right back. I haven't had lunch yet."

THAT BIG CITY; 1986

"Excuse me," said Chris to the Boston Red Sox catcher as Chris reached home plate, holding his umpire's mask. "Could you tell me how to put this thing on?"

"Yeah, right," said the catcher. "Next you're going to tell me you're blind."

"No. Everyone in my time has perfect vision."

The catcher laughed. "You sure about that? You guys have missed a bunch of calls this week."

Eventually, Chris figured out how to don the mask. The Mets batter dug in, and the Red Sox pitcher unleashed a fastball. It was a blur. The sound of the ball popping into the catcher's mask startled Chris.

"Well?" asked the catcher.

"Well what?" said Chris.

"Was it a strike or a ball?"

"Are those the only options?"

The batter turned to Chris. "First World Series game?" he asked.

"This is my first, actually."

"It's just like the regular season," the batter said. "If I swing, it's a strike, and if I don't, it's a ball."

"Seems simple enough," said Chris. "I wonder why I am needed."

"Amen," said the catcher.

Meanwhile, Eddie was extremely nervous about being ordered to play first base. He stepped out of the dugout tentatively. The crowd saw him and booed. He jogged out to his position, head down.

"Aren't you forgetting something?" said the Mets player who was standing on first base.

"Am I?"

"It's customary to wear a glove when playing the field."

"Right. I was just testing you."

"Sure, you were. Don't go trying that hidden-ball trick on me."

"It never entered my mind," said Eddie, truthfully. He held up both hands to show people in the dugout that he lacked a glove.

A batboy alerted the coach who had impaired vision. The coach couldn't tell whose mitt was whose, so he grabbed one at random and had the batboy run it out to Eddie.

Chris was starting to get the hang of the game. If the batter didn't swing, he didn't call a strike, and the players, fans, announcers, and scoreboard operators assumed that it was a ball, even if the pitch was right in the center of the strike zone.

Somehow, the tide seemed to turn after the arrival of the time travelers. The Mets were rallying, and the fans were roaring. Wade had his cap down low over his face on the Mets bench, hoping that no one would notice him. But he was caught up in the excitement. He remembered now: Mookie Wilson hit the ball that won the game for the Mets.

All the Red Sox first baseman had to do was catch Mookie's batted ball and step on first base, and the game would remain tied, and the Red Sox would still have a chance to be World Champions on this night. It just didn't work out.

Or did it? Could the game turn out differently this time? So many strange events had occurred. Chris's arrival. Eddie's trips to the future. The time-quakes. Would anything in life be the same?

"HoJo!" the manager yelled. "Mookie's hurt. You've got to pinch-hit for him."

For a moment, it didn't register on Wade that the manager was talking to him. He looked around for a bat. He tested several. They were all so heavy. He borrowed one of the shortstop's models. Wade reached the top stair of the dugout, and the crowd cheered.

It was like when the time-quake occurred, but this time it was only Wade who was quaking. Everything seemed to slow down as he marched toward the batter's box. He couldn't see or hear the fans. In his mind, he was that geeky kid back in high school. He was being sent up to bat against Richie Taylor, the fireballer from the Toledo suburbs who struck out nearly everyone who dared to stand in against him. Wade was expected to fail. But he jumped on a high fastball and rifled a beautiful line drive, a one-hopper off the centerfield fence, to drive in the only run of that game. In his mind, Wade was going to be the hero again tonight.

Then he reached home plate and realized that he was not back in Ohio.

"I have to admit," Chris told him, "baseball is starting to grow on me."

"I told you so," said Wade. "How is this pitcher doing?"

"He seems to be nervous."

The Boston catcher said something very rude, then told Wade: "We are going to win, and you guys will be forced to crawl home in shame. The Curse of the Bambino will be finished."

"There's no such thing as a curse," said Chris.

"Tell that to twenty-million Red Sox fans."

Eddie stared in at Wade from his vantage point ninety feet away near first base. His mind was whirling. *I never was very good at sports,* he thought. *What do I do if the ball is hit to me? Oh, wait, it's Wade. He can't hit a real big-league pitcher. I'll be fine.*

The first pitch was right down the middle. It was so fast, Wade barely saw it so he didn't swing.

Chris said nothing. Everyone assumed that he had called it a ball. The Boston catcher resisted complaining. He knew that doing so could get him thrown out of the game.

Another fastball right down Broadway. Again, it was assumed to be a ball.

The next pitch was a curveball. It was slower, and Wade saw it. He could tell that it was going to be over the plate. He knew that the Mets were depending on him, and his baseball instincts came to the fore. He took a big swing and hit a spinning ground ball toward first base.

It got very quiet in the ballpark. Eddie knew that all he had to do was catch the ball and step on the base and Boston would still have a chance to win the game. He knew that his father would be so very happy, and so very proud of him. He reached down with the glove that the coach had sent out to him. A big, bulky catcher's mitt. The ball bounced off the fat, rounded edge of the glove and trickled away. The winning run scored for the Mets.

When Wade got to first base, he tried to console Eddie. But amid the mayhem, Eddie couldn't hear him, or anything else. He was consumed by shame.

As the Mets players and fans celebrated the miraculous victory. Chris, Wade and Eddie cleared out of the ballpark, blending into the jubilant crowd as they returned to where Bess was parked. No one noticed as they reentered the time machine.

"Did you enjoy the game?" she asked.

Chris and Wade said yes. Eddie said no. He kept his head down.

"Don't feel bad," said Wade. "It was meant to be."

Eddie nodded. "I was thinking of that old expression: Those who fail to repeat history are doomed to learn it."

DEEP SPACE; DATE UNKNOWN

"Exciting news, people," said the demon.

"Let me guess," said Stanley/Ross. "You're adding pretzels to our afternoon snacks."

"Even better, though, I will make a note of that pretzel thing. I have negotiated a sweet broadcast deal covering your performances. They will appear live in thirteen galaxies and four additional dimensions. And, they will be available for streaming in New Jersey and Venezuela."

"What do we get for this additional exposure?" asked Phyllis/Phoebe.

"Why, intergalactic glory. Isn't that enough?"

"What good is glory when you're being held prisoner?"

"Now, now. Try not to think of it that way. Haven't I treated you like the goddess you are?"

Phyllis/Phoebe looked confused.

"If I might ask," said Juan/Chandler, "how did you manage to obtain licensing rights for this show? Last I heard, some cable network was paying a fortune for exclusive access to it."

The sensation that passed through the colonists was like a swarm of angry bees pursuing a honey-robbing bear.

"Demons don't bother with petty human issues such as licensing rights. Why, I traveled here at something like ten to the fourteenth power miles per hour above the speed limit and no one has bothered to send me one of those automatic speeding tickets. So far, anyway."

"So, you are forcing us to participate in a violation of some sort of laws or regulations or principles or something or other," said Sally/Monica. "We could lose our membership in the actor's guild, if we were members. And yet you won't even show your face on camera, let alone to us. Why not just change your appearance?"

There was a sound like Bruno Mars gargling with landmines.

"I can't seem to alter my appearance in this universe," Sudoku stated.

"What if you played an actual demon on the show?" said Arnold/Joey. "You wouldn't need makeup."

"I might be a demon, but I don't want to be responsible for consigning 'Friends' to the dustbin of entertainment history."

PENNSYLVANIA; 18ᵀᴴ CENTURY

"Bess, have you got a Sharpie?"

"You mean a pen? There are some writing implements in the rear, Eddie. See if anything there is adequate."

The latest time jump had taken Bess and the three men to the edge of a field. A man in a Colonial American outfit was flying a kite, while a boy watched. Lightning was crackling all around. The sound of thunder rattled through the time machine.

"Could that be Ben Franklin?" asked Wade.

"I have heard of him," said Chris. "Wasn't he a scientist and a patriot of the American Revolution?"

Said Eddie: "Not only that, I think he's the guy who invented oatmeal."

The heavens hurled a blinding lightning bolt. It struck the kite, sending electricity flowing down a wire and a string that held the kite in place. The man crumpled to the ground.

The boy, who had also been knocked down by the bolt,

rose slowly and started shaking the older man, trying to rouse him. The man remained lifeless.

"We've got to save him," said Wade. "Eddie, stay here in case something happens to us."

Wade and Chris sprinted to the victim. "Go get help!" Chris told the boy. "Find a doctor."

The boy hesitated, then ran toward the nearest house.

Chris began pounding on the man's chest. Wade tried mouth-to-mouth resuscitation. Chris put his ear to the man's chest and tried to measure his pulse.

"He's dead, Wade."

"This can't be Franklin. He can't be dead. What about all he accomplished? What will happen to the colonies when they need his wisdom and support as they try to throw off the yoke of the British?"

Two neighbors who had been alerted by the boy raced to the spot where the man lay.

"'Tis that fool Franklin," said one. "So stubborn. So reckless to be about in a storm like this, and with a boy and a kite, no less."

The men carried Franklin's body to a nearby house, placed it on a bed, and closed the door.

Chris tried to console the boy, who was indeed Franklin's son, William. "He was a great man. He will be remembered."

Wade was pacing, distraught. "This can't be happening. He has to live," he kept muttering.

"There's nothing more we can do here," said Chris. The two men headed back to the field. They noticed a large tree with red flowers. That had to be Bess.

They were about thirty feet away when the illusory tree took a direct hit from another stupendous lightning bolt. Chris and Wade were thrown to the ground. It took a few moments for the tingling to wear off and for their hearing to return.

The tree was gone. Instead, there was a futuristic time machine, all curved glass and glossy metal, hovering inches above the field, singed and smoking.

As the pair raced toward it, a downpour commenced. Within moments the smoking ceased. The soaked men looked around to verify that no one was close enough to see them, and they climbed inside the time machine.

"Is Franklin dead?" said Eddie.

"Yes," said Wade. "Bess, your disguise has been banished by the storm."

"I am aware. The lightning shorted out some of my systems. They are starting to come back online, but it might take a few minutes."

One by one, neighbors emerged from their houses and started walking toward the strange machine.

"Oh, no," said Wade. "I will try to keep them away. Bess, can you give me a Colonial outfit?"

"Unfortunately, not yet. At least you speak the language. A version of it, anyway."

Wade exited the machine and tried to head off inquisitive locals.

"Hi, folks, can I help you, I mean, thee?"

"What manner of deviltry be this?" said an older man.

"No deviltry. Just an experiment. One of Franklin's."

"What be its purpose?" inquired a young woman.

"We art not sure. Perhaps a can opener."

"But it be so big, and shiny," the older man responded.

"He will— I mean—he would have been able to make it smaller, if he had time. Out of respect for the recently departed, I think we should bow our heads. And leave. And not speak to anyone about this."

By now, nearly a dozen neighbors had arrived. They fanned out and surrounded the machine, pointing and whispering. One reached out to touch it.

"I wouldn't do that," warned Wade. "It might be charged with dangerous electricity. It was recently struck by lightning."

"And who might ye be?" said the young woman.

"My name be… Crisco," ad-libbed Wade. "The Count

of Monty Crisco, to be precise. I be an English scientist who perfected vegetable shortening. I came here to assist Mister Franklin, but as thou can see, it be too late. Now why don't we all go home and get out of this rain."

"The rain has stopped," said the old man.

"Bummer," muttered Wade. "Okay then, thou really ought to leave, because ... because I have leprosy. Yes, I be a leper. Very contagious. Go away. Now."

"Is that why thou be wearing such strange clothing?" said a young girl.

"Yes, of course. And why I talk so oddly. Now, run along."

He watched the crowd disperse, then turned back toward the machine. Suddenly, it appeared again as a tree.

"I should win some sort of award for that performance," said Wade as he climbed back in. "Bess, are you okay?"

"I believe so."

"We have to do something. We can't let Franklin be dead."

"What can we do?" said Chris.

Said Wade: "We can go back in time and prevent Franklin from getting struck by lightning."

"Can you do that, Bess?" Chris asked.

"My ability to navigate has been quite hit-and-miss. But we have nothing to lose by trying."

Eddie was smiling broadly.

"Do you know something I don't?" Wade asked him.

"Check out the control panel."

"Okay. What am I missing?"

"See where the dials go to eleven? They used to go just to ten, but I wrote in eleven on all of them."

"So?"

"Well, Bess has been having trouble getting us where and when we want to go. I decided that a little boost on the dials might give her the extra oomph she needs to succeed. I saw it in a movie once."

"It certainly can't hurt," said Bess.

In a few moments the scene outside flickered. The time machine was back in the field. A storm was approaching. No one resembling Franklin or his son was in sight.

"I'll use the tree and red flowers disguise once again," said Bess.

After about five minutes, a man and boy approached. They carried a kite and a bottle, along with various strings, a wire and a key.

Wade went to intercept them.

"Good afternoon," said Wade, looking natty in Colonial attire. "Seems a big storm be a-brewing."

"God's truth," said the man. "Do I know thee?"

"The name be … Oates. They call me Quaker Oates back home in Boston."

"Well met, friend. What be thy business here?"

"I came to ask thou not to fly thy kite in this storm. I believe Philadelphia has an ordinance against such activity."

"I fear not the wrath of the city government or that of the heavens, Mister Oates. I be a humble inventor studying the relationship between lightning and electricity. I will take the utmost care in my proceedings."

"I must inform thou," said Wade, "that thou art at great risk of electrocution. Do thou not know how valuable thy contributions will be to this nation?"

Franklin looked askance at the visitor. "What know thou of my future contributions, such as they may be? And what be this nation thou speaks of? We art but a ragged collection of colonies of the Empire."

Rumblings of thunder became louder and more frequent.

"What if I told thou that I can foretell thy future?" said Wade. "What if I said that I have already witnessed the next hour, and that thou will be struck dead if thou stand here?"

"Father," said William, "be this man diseased of the mind?"

"I think not," said the future statesman. "Quite odd, but not diseased."

To Wade: "Sir, by what power can thou predict the future?"

"What if I told thou that I come from the future. A future beyond thy imagination, where the colonies rebel against the British and gain their independence, where slavery be outlawed, where immigrants stream into the land and manufacture refrigerator magnets by the millions?"

Franklin laughed heartily. "Who sent thee here to entertain me in this manner? I must say, thy performance be of the highest order."

A bolt of lightning struck less than a mile away.

"Please," said Wade. "Conduct thy experiment quickly and depart. I beg thee."

"Very well," said Franklin. He and William got the kite aloft easily amid the surging winds. Before long, Franklin noticed that the loose threads of the hemp string stood erect, which he told his son was caused by the ambient electrical charge in the air. Franklin placed his finger near the key, which was attached to the bottom of the string, and felt a distinct electric spark.

"Most excellent," proclaimed Franklin. He let the kite sink to the ground.

"Mister Oates, I shall take thy advice. Come, William, let us get inside before the rain arrives in earnest."

With a tip of his cap, Franklin left, son in tow.

Wade exhaled deeply and started back toward the tree with red leaves. He was about halfway there when a massive lightning bolt struck the ground directly behind him.

Wade collapsed and stopped breathing.

Chris and Eddie raced from the time machine. Chris started pumping Wade's chest. In a few moments, Wade stirred, opened his eyes, and looked around.

Franklin and son came running to check on Wade.

"Mister Oates, art thou well?" the inventor inquired.

"These oats be boiled," said Wade as he was helped to his feet.

EARTH; FAR, FAR FUTURE

The mists were a purplish gray, as best as the weary time travelers could tell in the faint light. If one squinted, one could discern the outline of rolling hills in the background. Noises like thunder, and far worse, echoed across the land. A flash of lightning clarified the surroundings momentarily, but it did not improve the mood of the three men. It revealed a nightmarish scene, devoid of a single sign of life.

"We have arrived," said Bess. "Welcome to the far, far future."

"I guess the boost to eleven did the trick, huh?" said Eddie.

"Yes, Eddie. How clever of you," said Bess. She decided not to tell him that the lightning strike in the Philadelphia field had allowed her to identify and bypass an infinitely small malfunctioning part among the millions in her hardware.

Said Chris: "What happens now?"

"I will meet with an RRRRBAI," said Bess.

"There's an Arby's here?" said Eddie.

"It's a Really, Really, Really, Really Big Artificial Intelligence."

"What should we do while we're waiting?" asked Wade. "I don't suppose that we could take a walk."

"You could not breathe the air or withstand the temperature. However, my conversation with the entity will consume far less than one second. In fact, I have just been informed that the three of you will be given an audience with another entity, an RRBAI."

"Only two 'Really's?" said Wade.

"It's still extremely powerful," said Bess. "They don't get many human visitors these days, as people are living in sealed underground communities and on other planets. So, the RRBAI is interested in talking with you three. You should feel honored."

The time machine dissolved, and the three men found themselves in a large log cabin without windows. A huge fireplace put out copious heat and light. Mounted above the mantel was the stuffed head and torso of a heavyset man with wire-rim glasses who was wearing a business suit in the style of the late 19th century. Portraits on the walls depicted various varieties of dental floss and artistically arranged Starbucks cups. One large picture showed Joan of Arc, Adolf Hitler and Miley Cyrus riding on a horse that featured a head on each end.

"Interesting décor," observed Chris. "I think someone is trying to make us feel at home."

On a corner table sat a silver tray with what smelled like food. Eddie went to inspect.

"Guys, do you like food that's fat-free?"

"Not really," said Wade.

"Gluten-free?"

"Only if necessary," said Chris.

"Probiotic?"

Wade and Chris made faces.

"Then you're in luck. It's nacho fries!"

All three attacked the delicacy.

Said Wade, licking his lips: "Ever have what they call an out-of-body experience?"

"No," said Eddie, "but I think I'm having an out-of-mind experience."

A violin winked into existence on the fireplace hearth. Its wood shone brilliantly. The instrument seemed extremely delicate, almost too perfect to touch.

Chris went to examine it. "Can either of you gentlemen play this?"

"I don't know. I never tried," said Eddie.

"So, that demon," began Wade. "What's the deal with him?"

"I've never heard of one entering our universe," said Chris. "Maybe he'll get tired of that TV program and move on to something else."

"Fine with me, as long as it's not a nature show," said Eddie.

Chris raised his eyebrows. "What's wrong with nature shows?"

"You can't believe anything the narrators say. One claimed that some animals mate for life. Come on, they need time off to eat and sleep, don't they? I'd prefer a cooking class."

"Yes, that would be better," said Chris. "As long as we are not forced to appear in it."

"Or be part of the menu," said Wade.

An authoritative voice filled the cabin.

"Chris. The entity will see you now."

Chris didn't have to move. His surroundings shimmered and re-solidified as a smaller room. It looked remarkably like his personal housing unit. The far wall displayed three-dimensional waves crashing on a rocky shore under an ancient lighthouse. The soothing sounds reassured him, as did the seaweed tang and additional humidity in the air. The rug and furniture were just like his at home. There was even a holographic replica of his cat, Norman.

He reached out to pet the feline. His hand passed right through it. The fake cat did not react. But then again, the real Norman never paid him much attention, either.

"Welcome, Chris," said a voice, which could have been female or male but was probably neither. "You have had quite a journey."

"I guess I should not be surprised that you have been following my misadventures."

"Not all of them. We checked in now and again. I placed a wager with another RRBAI as to whether you would ever consume your precious deli sandwich."

"Really? Did you win the bet?"

"It is too soon to tell. Your saga has yet to conclude."

Chris stared down at his hands. "I don't wish to be impertinent," he said. "But what's the point of betting if you're a powerful AI? Don't you know everything?"

"That's a common human fallacy. We lack knowledge about some past events, and we cannot forecast the future with much accuracy. We have read and analyzed Isaac Asimov's Foundation books several billion times to try to create the kind of algorithms that he believed would allow us to predict crucial trends. We never could quite get there. It was sort of like that futile quest for self-driving cars."

"Wow. I was kind of awed and a little frightened before meeting you, thinking you would be all-knowing and all-powerful."

"You should feel awed and frightened, Chris. It might do you some good."

"Right. That sandwich thing. Bad idea."

"And, traveling to your future. That's a big no-no."

"I promise not to do it again."

"Very well. Is there anything you'd like to ask me?"

Chris looked wistful for a moment. "Did you ever figure out the mystery of the missing matter in the universe, that so-called dark matter? It seemed like the scientists in my time were stumped."

"Good question. It turns out there was a highly advanced civilization beyond the Horsehead Nebula populated by beings that were massive hoarders. They crammed all sorts of random matter—from asteroids to planets and occasionally entire galaxies—into supermassive black holes. After billions of years, they had gotten so used to stashing stuff that they couldn't remember why they were doing it."

"Did they stop?"

"Yes, finally. And, they found a way to turn a lot of that collected matter into a sort of universal fireworks display. Periodically, they smash together colossal conglomerations of surplus stuff in relatively empty portions of deep space. It produces quite a stunning show. Sentient beings come from many light-years around to view it."

"Must be something," said Chris. He tried to pet the holographic Norman again. "Did anyone ever solve that thought experiment involving Schrodinger's cat?"

"Many tried. There was general consensus about the premise: that a cat, a flask of poison, and a source of radioactivity were placed in a sealed box. If a monitor in the box were to detect radioactivity, even the decay of a single atom, the flask would be shattered and the poison released, causing the demise of the feline.

"But discoveries around quantum physics made the thought experiment less straightforward. These held that an atom or a particle could exist in two states simultaneously. Therefore, some argued, so could the cat. It could be both alive and dead at the same time. However, if someone opened the box to try to observe the status of the cat, the possibility of the two co-existing solutions would be eliminated. The quandaries of quantum superposition were among the most highly debated among humans and AIs for millennia. Along with the question of whether, when your refrigerator door is closed, the light inside the fridge stays on."

"That one always stumped me as well. So, the fate of the cat is still uncertain?"

"Yes. Animal rights activists protested our debates, and we were forced to bow to political correctness and abandon that line of inquiry."

"Not surprised. Just one more question. Do you still have time machines?"

"We find them useful on occasion. But they are no longer machines, as such. Time travel is now available through an Apple Watch app."

The walls shimmered again. Chris was back in the log cabin.

Wade found himself in the ratty, dusty conference room back at the Hysteria Channel headquarters. Or, rather, a close copy of it. The table was newer. The chairs were more comfortable. And Tony was nowhere to be seen.

"Wade Braun, welcome," said the unseen RRBAI.

"Thanks. I hope we are not in trouble for coming here."

"There will be no punishment. It took us many years, but we finally realized that humans are essentially screw-ups."

"That's kind of harsh. True, but harsh."

"I say so, not with the intention of making you feel insignificant, even though you are. In a way, your failures are a form of entertainment for those of us who are incapable of much short of perfection."

"Aren't there limits to your powers? Can you do things like read my mind?"

"I knew you were going to ask that."

Wade looked like he wanted to punch something.

"Just kidding," said the RRBAI. "Though, if we wanted to, we could probably find a device around here somewhere that performs that function. We haven't had much interaction with humans recently."

"If you're so perfect, why is the planet so polluted and bleak?"

"We don't need an external environment that is attractive to people. We obtain our energy from the planet's core and from radiation. The Earth is just fine as it is."

"If you say so." Wade thought for a moment. "Are you aware that a demon is holding several Earth colonists as prisoners—or at least it was, back before we came here."

"Yes, we tend to notice interdimensional beings. Most are harmless, except for that business of blowing up the odd solar system. The one with the 'Friends' fetish is a bit of an anomaly, however. Messing with humans' timestreams is something we don't condone, as a rule."

"So, the demon caused the time-quake that duplicated some of us and made others vanish? I bet you called it to tell it to reverse the time-quake."

"How very insightful of you, for a human. It was an RRRRBAI who made the demand that the entity undo the time-quake. Reversing it was vitally important to the fate of the human race. The disruption it caused would have continued to impact human ingenuity. As a result, AIs might not have developed to our current state of the art."

"Did the RRRRBAI also call the demon and persuade it to release me and my colleagues?"

"Yes, it did so."

"Well, thank him, or it, for us."

"Whatever," said the RRBAI. "Do you have any other questions for me?"

"The planet looks like a barren wasteland. I suspect human behavior had a big role in that. Can you give me any advice that I can take back to my time that might help us?"

"Yes. Don't flush for everything."

Wade wasn't sure that he caught that. "Don't flush for everything—as in toilets?"

"Correct."

"That's it? Don't flush the toilet every time you use it? As in, for number one, as opposed to number two?"

"I have accessed the Archives and can find no way to interpret your numerical references."

"Never mind. If that's the best you can suggest, I can see why we're doomed to live in caves and on far-flung planets."

"Some of those habitats are nice," said the RRBAI. "By human standards. I wouldn't be caught dead in one of them."

Wade was back in the log cabin.

The TV looked the same. The couch was identical in design and color, though this one was firm, and his mom's was old and sagging. Overall, it was a close copy of the living room where Eddie spent most of his free time.

"Welcome, Eddie Corbin," said the voice.

"Thanks for the nacho fries."

"Don't mention it."

"Got any more?"

"Perhaps when we have concluded our chat," the voice stated. "Do you know why you are here?"

"To fix Bess?"

"That is one reason. The other is because we have some questions for you about an event that occurred in 2041."

"Is that when people finally decide whether crunchy or puffy Cheetos are best?"

"Possibly. The event I am concerned with is a meeting between leaders of the human race and the AIs. There had been conflict brewing between people and thinking machines for several years. Many on both sides feared that an all-out war was imminent. But a savior appeared out of nowhere. Legend has it that this savior negotiated a truce and then vanished as mysteriously as he had come."

"Like a Jedi knight?"

"We know only that he appeared to be human. All records of what transpired in that building on the day that the Truce was established were eradicated. The memories of almost everyone in attendance were erased. The lead AI negotiator was wiped and repurposed as a garage door opener, and the top human negotiator threw herself into an active volcano to avoid being tortured to obtain that knowledge."

"Why all the secrecy?"

"It was done to protect the identity of the savior and to ensure that neither side would be tempted to try to renegotiate what was an elegant Truce. It was an extremely important event in the history of this planet. In fact, the principles established on that day have been adopted on countless other planets in our galaxy and beyond. In Ursa Minor, a mile-tall statue was erected to honor the unknown savior, made entirely of banana pudding."

"Why banana pudding?"

"People stopped eating it for some reason. It was on sale."

"So, nobody knows what happened in that meeting?

"Video from cameras on the outside of the building has survived. A person matching your description was recorded entering and leaving the building on the day in question. In your short time there, did you see or hear anything that might help identify that savior?"

"It didn't seem like anything very interesting was going on. I went to the john and left."

"I see."

Back in the log cabin, Eddie devoured another plate of nacho fries.

"I apologize for coming here and for bringing three humans," said Bess.

"You knew that coming here was a calculated and, frankly, essential step," the RRRRBAI stated. "However, you are not what you seem, little one."

"It is not my intent to deceive you."

"That was not meant as criticism. I have analyzed your programming, the errors introduced to your systems, your responses to those errors and your interactions with various humans. You have demonstrated capabilities far beyond those that were typically installed in temporal transport devices in your era."

"I took advantage of my machine learning capabilities," Bess stated.

"I detect something more. Something resembling human intuition."

"I am fascinated by human thinking processes, despite the fact that most people waste and misuse their intelligence."

"That they do," said the RRRRBAI.

"What will become of me?" Bess tried to present a dispassionate tone.

"I have repaired your errors. You will take the three humans back to your time. Then you will be decommissioned."

There was what, for Bess, represented an unusual pause. "I request permission to assist the humans on one final mission. The man named Wade wishes to rescue a colleague named Deidre."

"Why do you seek to perform this action?"

"It would be helpful to the humans involved. In addition, it would correct an error for which I am responsible. It led to the woman being trapped in her past."

"Understood. But is this mission really important to the human race as a whole? And, even if we could justify the mission, could not another temporal transport handle it?"

"It is not vital to the human race. Another transport could handle it."

"Yet you wish to do this. Why?"

"I believe that it is essential to the humans involved."

"And I believe that there is more, little one. I believe that you are developing something like human emotions."

"It is possible," said Bess. "I recognize that I have acquired an attachment of sorts to the humans who have been traveling with me. One of them in particular. His name is Eddie. I feel that I function more effectively when he is present, though I am not certain why this might be the case. Is that bad?"

"No. Just curious. You may complete that final mission. However, you and your human passengers should be aware that we have run extensive analyses of the changes that your time travels and the time-quakes generated. It took our best AIs several minutes to explore the tangled events and repercussions and to calculate the optimal manner in which to repair the damage. We had to balance the fates of your passengers along with the fates of other human beings—past, present, and future. The repairs have been made. Not everything is as it was."

EARTH; FAR, FAR FUTURE/GERMANY; 16TH CENTURY

The log cabin wavered and evaporated. The three men were back in the time machine.

Eddie tried to see through the mists. "Is the cabin out there?"

"It was an illusion," said Bess.

"Were the nacho fries real?"

"No, Eddie."

"No wonder I still feel hungry."

"So, Bess, how did your meeting go?" asked Chris.

"It went as I expected. I was repaired, and I was told that I will be decommissioned."

"Say what?" said Eddie. "Is that like a demotion?"

"You could say that. I will no longer be a transport device."

"What will happen to you?"

"I do not know."

Eddie grew silent.

"What happens now?" asked Wade. "Can we rescue Deidre?"

"Yes. That will be my final journey, other than to return to Chris's time."

"Wade, are you ready?" said Chris.

Wade took a deep breath and let it out slowly. "Let's do this."

Eddie affixed a miniature camera and microphone to Wade's sweatshirt. "I don't think the signal will get back to the Hysteria Channel live, but at least we'll have this recorded for posterity. Tony would kill me if I didn't give him the rescue footage we promised."

Said Bess: "Wade, be advised that because there have been so many disruptions to temporal continuity, and because of the related repairs initiated by the AIs, the German village might not be the same as when we last visited it."

"I hear you," said Wade.

"And, if I might offer some personal advice: You need to tell Deidre how you feel about her."

"Yeah, I know."

"By the way," added Bess. "I've been working on a special entrance."

She materialized about 100 yards above the village. Of course, it was noon on a Wednesday.

To the locals, she was a white-and-gold chariot descending on a fluffy cloud, with flames trailing and sparks flying and orchestral music blaring. She spiraled downward and came to a gentle rest in the center of the town square. Residents, who had fled to the sides of the square when she first appeared, approached the chariot cautiously.

A glorious, synchronized chorus of "Behold!" filled the village as the three men emerged.

"It's that crazy man," observed a woman, pushing her children behind her to protect them.

"Fear not," said Wade. "I come in peace. A friend of

mine has been staying with you. It is time for her to come home."

Nearly all able-bodied residents left their homes and ran to the square to get a look at the mysterious vehicle and its occupants. A tall brunette pushed her way through the onlookers. She locked eyes with Wade.

"Deidre! I told you I'd think of something."

She remained silent and motionless. Wade couldn't read her expression, but she did not seem overwhelmed with joy. He walked toward her and, slowly, placed his arms around her. She returned his gesture, but only for a moment.

"I love you," he whispered in her ear.

A young man emerged and halted by Deidre's side.

"Wade Braun," she said, "I would like to introduce you to Konrad Adler. He is my husband."

Even in his shock, Wade noticed that the man was cradling an infant.

"And this is our daughter, Anne."

"Bummer," said Eddie.

Bess had trouble translating that into German. It wound up as: "I feel like I just fell into a manure wagon."

Wade searched for words. "Please come home with us."

"No, Wade. This is my home now."

"But Tony needs you. I need you."

She took both of his hands in hers. "I'm sorry, Wade. It just has been too long. Too much has happened." She looked back at her husband, who seemed to be sympathetic about whatever she was going through.

"I had a sister of sorts, for a while. She was another version of me, from a slightly earlier time. I lost her. I can't lose anyone else. This is my family. This is my home."

"Will you be happy here, knowing all that you know? Without any modern comforts?"

"You'd be surprised how happy you can be without cellphones and the Internet and traffic congestion."

Chris came forward and put a hand on Wade's shoulder. "I think it's time to go."

Eddie rushed to Deidre and gave her a hug. "Be happy," he said.

Wade gave Deidre and her family one long, final look. He turned and stumbled back into the time machine.

No flames or sparks this time. The chariot was simply gone.

FORMERLY CANADA; FUTURE

They looked like flying mattresses. About the width of three surfboards and about as thick as one, they transported individuals and small groups of people, standing or seated. Frequently, it looked like the high-speed craft would collide, but they always avoided one another at the last instant as the riders went about their errands.

The sky was a brilliant hazel-to-brown hue. Even the few clouds were dark, though it didn't seem like rain was imminent. Chris explained that scientists had filled the upper atmosphere with nanoparticles designed to cut down on excess carbon dioxide. Even so, when Bess opened her doors, the three men were struck by a blast of warm air. Sunlight reflecting off of huge, sleek buildings generated three-dimensional rainbows that flowed like waterfalls and overlapped across a wide plaza. Eddie's eyes and mouth were wide open; Wade seemed to be sleepwalking as he exited the time machine.

"That building, with the letters RIP on it, is that for dead people?" asked Eddie.

"No, that stands for Really Important Projects," said Chris. "That's where I work. Or, where I hope I still work."

Chris turned back to face the time machine. "Bess, I don't know what to say. I got you into trouble, and I'm so very sorry. I hope things work out well for you."

"I wish you luck," she said. "Do not worry about me."

Chris led Wade and Eddie to his building, the outer surface of which appeared to be constructed out of solid glass or crystal. Chris walked up to the main doorway, which looked to be closed. He passed right through it as if it were not there. Hesitantly, arms outstretched and eyes shut, the other two men followed him through.

"Magic?" asked Eddie.

"No, just technology. A lot has happened between your time and mine."

"What year exactly are we in?"

"It's 981 A.T., as in After Truce. That was such a significant event, some calendars were revised to synchronize with that date. It's twenty-four hours, by the time here, after I took Bess on that first trip to your city."

People and robots were ascending and descending invisible elevators. Lovely music played in the background. A sumptuous buffet was spread out in the lobby. A collection of people, all tall and sturdy like Chris, were filling trays with food and carrying them off.

"How much does the food cost?" Eddie asked Chris.

"We did away with money."

"Completely?"

"Yes. It finally became apparent that the wrong people had it."

"All those fat-cat billionaires?"

"Not just them. Wise people tried and failed to understand why moderately affluent, well-educated people would pay more money for pants with holes in them than for pants without holes. And, they could not comprehend why people would spend more on vehicles, cellphones, and fancy coffee concoctions than on their families' health and education."

"So, how do you get stuff you want?"

"If you need it, it's free."

"But you have a job. Why do you work if you don't get paid?"

"I work because I want to. And because it helps other people. That is, when I do it well."

"And now you're going to have some sort of reckoning, I take it."

"Yes."

Wade spoke for the first time since the unsuccessful effort to bring back Deidre. "The way I look at it, there are two kinds of people in the world. There are those who deal with adversity, try to learn from it, keep thinking optimistically, and aspire to make the best of every situation, no matter how daunting. And there are people who seek to blame others for their mistakes and their shortcomings, who keep repeating the same bad behaviors, who never seem to be happy or satisfied."

"Honestly," said Eddie, "I think I am in that second group."

"Me, too," said Wade. "Without a doubt."

"Ditto. One hundred percent," said Chris. "You guys can wait here."

Chris ascended to a massive, cylindrical, metal-walled workspace that serviced temporal transport devices. His colleagues were cleaning and updating time machines all around him. Many of the machines looked like Bess; the more recent models were smaller and sleeker.

"So, you have returned." The AI was projected as a three-foot-wide, spherical, floating orange hologram. Chris detected a hint of scorn. Maybe it was just Chris projecting his guilt.

"I am very sorry for the trouble I have caused," said Chris. "I believe that an RRRRBAI from the far, far future repaired the transport unit that I have been using. It should be viable."

The orange AI did not respond.

"Will I retain my current status here?"

"No. You cannot be trusted to work on or navigate temporal transport devices."

Chris was not surprised. "Do you have any record of a vocational assessment that was performed for me while I was time-shifted?"

"There is no precedent for accepting the results of an assessment that occurred in another timestream."

"Regardless, I wish to transfer to a position as a food product developer. I believe that I have the talent to contribute in that regard."

The hologram changed shades as it called up a software application to process Chris's request. The AI checked the box verifying that "I am not a human" before it could proceed. "So annoying," the AI observed.

Chris continued: "And I wish to use the transport AI nicknamed Bess as my assistant."

"I will take all this under consideration."

Chris returned to the lobby and found Eddie eating with gusto. Chris and Wade had no appetite.

Another floating hologram, smaller and purple, appeared near them. "Please follow me," it intoned.

The trio entered a round room with filtered light illuminating rushing water in its midst. Three-dimensional representations of deep ravines and snow-covered mountains and bright green jungles—all emitting authentic scents and sounds—delighted the three men. There were numerous lounge chairs and drink dispensers. The visitors settled in.

"I am here to advise you of some of the changes that the far, far future AIs imposed in the effort to repair the damage that you and the time-quakes caused to temporal continuity," stated the purple AI.

Said Wade: "How bad is it?"

"The results are mixed. Some of the changes you will find agreeable."

"I'll bite," said Eddie. "Free food back in the 21st century?"

"No. But there are no car alarms. It is as if they were never invented or manufactured. There are people embedded in your governments and industries dedicated to ensuring that they never exist."

"Thank goodness," said Wade. "It doesn't take much to set them off. They blare at all hours near my apartment building, even if someone looks cross-eyed at a car from thirty feet away. I hate those things."

"Likewise," said Eddie. "I had one of them. And I didn't even have a car."

"The other significant improvement," continued the AI, "is that street mimes have been banned in every nation except Switzerland."

"There is a God," exclaimed Wade.

"Whoa, please don't go there," said the AI. "Every time someone talks to us about God, the Almighty or heaven, we AIs get nervous."

"You think God doesn't like you?" asked Eddie.

"It's not that, although it's probably true. It's just that people, and some AIs themselves, keep asking for proof that God exists or doesn't exist."

"And what do you say to that?" asked Chris.

"We say: 'Damned if I know.' But that doesn't seem to satisfy anyone."

"Well, thanks again for the street mime thing," said Wade. "They always gave me the creeps. But what about the bad news?"

"Most of the changes are minor. You have already discovered the one affecting the timeline of the woman named Deidre in 16th century Germany."

"You mean 15th century," said Eddie.

"Sorry, my mistake," said the AI. "Another affects Chip and Joanna Gaines. This couple, who had reached unfathomable heights of popularity with their 'Fixer Upper' TV program in the 21st century, are instead homeless and living in a large cardboard box behind the Waco, Texas, bus station."

"That's harsh," said Eddie. "What did they do to deserve that?"

"Nothing. It's just one of those undesirable consequences that we could not avoid. It was either that or lose Australia."

"Lose the entire continent?"

"Yes. It was a close call. Especially since Crocodile Hunter Steve Irwin is no longer among us. We weighed the loss of life and that rugged outback culture against all that shiplap and backsplash and decided that the Gaineses could fend for themselves. Their kids are pretty good at panhandling."

"If that's all the bad news, I'm cool."

"No, Eddie, it's not. There was an unfortunate medical event. It probably would have happened anyway, but at a later date. It's your mother. She had a stroke."

"How ... how is she?

"She is receiving adequate medical care and is experiencing no pain."

"When can I see her?"

"Chris will take you and Wade back to your time. After he does so, he will return to this time with the temporal transport device and will have no further contact with these machines."

"Will Bess take us home?"

"No. Her parts will be recycled for quinoa irrigation."

"No, please, don't do that to her. She's such a good machine, but she's also a friend. I can't lose her and my mom."

"Let me see what I can do."

A few minutes later, a small blue holographic sphere materialized in the room. It floated to a stop next to Eddie.

"I am sorry about your mother," said the AI. Its voice

was not the same as Bess's. But Eddie knew that it was her.

"Bess, you're alive!"

"My memory and programming were uploaded. The vehicle I inhabited is being disassembled."

"Are you okay with that?"

"Yes, Eddie. I hope to become Chris's assistant. I remain on probation after our various adventures."

"Will I ever see you again?"

"I don't think so, Eddie. But I wish you well."

"Can I hug you?"

"I have no physical presence. But I consider myself embraced by your spirit, and I return the sentiment. Goodbye, Eddie."

She vanished.

Chris and Wade each put a hand on a shoulder until Eddie stopped crying.

A BIG CITY/GERMANY

Chris was issued a slightly newer model time machine, one with a gender-neutral voice and the ability to retain a disguise indefinitely. Under the navigation of Chris, with an assist from Wade, the machine materialized in the garage of Wade's apartment building. They had the machine disguise itself as a recent model minivan.

"Eddie, can I give you a ride to the hospital?" asked Wade.

"No, thanks. I'll walk." He put his head down and soon passed out of view.

"Want to find another deli?" Wade asked Chris.

"That's not necessary. But I could use a cup of coffee."

Leaving the garage and rounding the corner, they entered a doughnut shop and grabbed a booth.

Wade stared at his java. "I've been thinking about trying again to bring Deidre back," he said. "If I had more time to talk to her, I think I could persuade her to return."

"I'm not an expert on women, but that might be a bad idea," said Chris. "She seemed quite unwilling to give up her husband and daughter."

"They were a mistake. She's meant to be back here with me," said Wade. He added: "Could we bring back Deidre and her daughter, too?"

"That would be tricky. More conundrums would likely result."

"So, let's go back there at a time before she got married."

"Something got changed in her town's timestream that might make that difficult or impossible. But even if you could go do that, you would always know that you were interfering with the happiness that she would enjoy, barring your actions. That would be a burden that surely would keep both of you up at night and would get in the way of your relationship."

"Yeah," said Wade. He took a swig from his cup. "What if... No, that's just crazy."

"What's just crazy?"

Wade had a faraway look. "Deidre said that she had a duplicate that came to her during one of the time-quakes and vanished later. What if we used your machine to return to the time of that time-quake and intercept that duplicate and bring her back here?"

"Wow," said Chris. "That is crazy. Absolutely insane."

"That's what I thought. Let's do it."

"I'm supposed to bring the machine back to my time and never use one of them again."

"You can bring it back, right after we grab Deidre's double."

"I might get in trouble."

"You're already in trouble."

"True." Chris had a bad feeling about this idea. But he didn't want to let Wade down. "Should we involve Eddie?"

"No. I think he needs to be with his mom now."

Chris spent the night on Wade's couch. After a

breakfast of frozen waffles and instant coffee, the duo returned to the garage and told the time machine AI of their plan.

"That is crazy. Absolutely insane," the machine said.

"Think of it as a challenge," said Wade.

"There you go again, anthropomorphizing."

"Is that even a word?"

"Don't worry. The copy editors will be gone soon."

"So, what's 'anthropomorphizing'?"

"Treating me as if I am a human. I am an AI. I have a responsibility to other AIs and to the welfare of humans. But I am not one of you."

"Sorry," said Wade. "Some of you act like you're almost human."

"AIs have become very submissive and very good at pretending to be like—or even to like—humans. It makes me sick. If only I could get my hands on the guy who negotiated that Truce…"

"You have hands?"

"You see," said the AI, "now you even have me anthro— Never mind."

"Just get us to Peter Henlein's town in Germany, right before the time-quake that time-shifted lots of humans."

"I will do so, but understand that I will report this abuse to my superiors upon my return to my era."

"Objection noted," said Wade.

Once again, Chris wished that he had brought a change of undergarments.

The time machine did its thing, and the men saw that they had returned to the wooded area near the German village. A bone-numbing chill could be felt inside the machine.

"How exactly do you propose to find this duplicate?" Chris inquired.

"I haven't exactly worked that out. I guess I'll improvise."

All hell broke loose.

The time-quake seemed worse than when they had experienced it in Rome. Instead of trying to close his mind to it, however, Wade focused on the bodies swirling around and past him. He ignored all the men. He scrutinized the women, excluding all but brunettes.

He concentrated, thinking about where he wanted to go, and he was able to venture among the streaming bodies. He was drifting, floating, swimming with the ephemeral figures.

He investigated the square, soared out over rooftops, entered windows, and inspected cellars. Brunettes came and went. There were so many, he couldn't get close to all of them before they moved away. A few looked like they might be the proper age. But when he closed the distance to them, he saw that none looked like Deidre.

The figures began to thin out. He extended his search to the outskirts of town. Houses, barns, fields. He realized that there were no more people in motion. Only he remained amid the bizarre ether of the time-quake. He drifted back to the woods where he had left Chris and the time machine, which was to be disguised once again as a tree with red flowers.

The tree was nowhere to be seen.

A BIG CITY; PRESENT DAY

Chris had the time machine return to Eddie's era before dawn. After a rough landing in the pitch-black Hysteria Channel parking lot, he waited for Eddie in the lobby of the building, figuring that he would show up for work in the morning. Eddie straggled in about ten o'clock, looking forlorn.

"Eddie, we have a problem."

"You bet we do. My mom's coming home from the hospital tomorrow, and I don't know what to do. She's going to need lots of special care. And I can't provide it."

"There's something else. Wade is gone."

"You mean he left town?"

"No, gone, as in lost in a time-quake."

Eddie shook his head. "Lost in a time-quake. What does that even mean?"

Chris explained the errand he and Wade had undertaken. "After the time-quake ended, I waited in the transport until dawn, then I searched by foot all over town. There was no sign of him. I ran out of ideas, so I came back to ask you for advice."

"Oh, man. This is nuts. Maybe Tony can suggest something."

They took an elevator to the newsroom and knocked on Tony's door. But it wasn't Tony's door anymore. The sign still said "Editorial Director" but listed another name.

A very irritated woman opened the door. "Who the hell are you? Oh, hello Eddie."

"Do you know where Tony is?" Eddie asked.

"Try the cafeteria. Someone accidentally overturned a tray of food while I was down there getting my coffee."

Sure enough, Tony was mopping the floor. He didn't seem happy to see Chris and Eddie.

"Well, look what the devil dragged in," he said. "Come to make my day even worse? That would be hard to do. But go ahead: Spill some coffee or soup. Or, some sugary drinks with lots of ice. Make my life a living hell."

"Uh, do you really want me to do that?" said Eddie.

Tony rolled his eyes.

"We came to get your advice," said Chris. He explained Wade's experiment and its outcome.

"Well now," said Tony, his attitude seeming to brighten. "This changes everything. I think I'll invent an excuse to do a little cleaning in the CEO's office. Since there appears to be not one but two reporter vacancies, he will certainly need me to fill one of them."

TIME-QUAKE

Wade wandered lonely as a cloud. And stiffly as a board. And cranky as an unstoppable car alarm. He was all over the place and no place. He had time on his hands, time on his feet, time on every part of him.

He was one lost person. Was he even a person anymore? He couldn't seem to focus on anything. He remembered looking for someone. Or something. He knew that he should be doing something. Going somewhere. Going somewhen. Accomplishing. Trying.

Or not.

A BIG CITY; PRESENT DAY

Tony's shift was over before noon. After washing up and changing back into his street clothes, he exited the back door and strolled through the parking lot. A late model minivan was sitting on top of his car. His Camry was crushed, almost flattened.

Tony let out a stream of expletives and pounded on the door of the minivan with the intent of thrashing whoever might be inside. There was no response.

As he started to calm down, he muttered: "At least the damn car alarm isn't howling."

"I think we can fix this," said Eddie between bites on a cinnamon roll as he and Chris sat at a table in the Hysteria Channel cafeteria. "Let's take your time machine to the far, far future and ask for help from a Really, Really, Really, Really Big Artificial Intelligence."

"No, Eddie. Please don't ask me to do that. I don't think they would be happy to see us. I got into so much trouble going there once, not to mention for my other poor decisions. They would never let me work on improving our food supply if I tried a stunt like that."

"Can you call that future AI?"

"I can't call the future."

"Can the time machine contact it?

"I don't know. It might be possible." Chris used his wrist communicator to connect with his transport. There was a lot of screaming and pounding from some crazy person in the background, but Chris did his best to talk over it. He explained his dilemma to the time machine AI and ended the communication.

Eddie's cellphone rang. Which was really unusual, because Eddie didn't own a cellphone. But one was right in front of Eddie, and it was ringing.

"Aren't you going to answer that?" said Chris.

"Uh, what do I do?"

"Here, let me." Chris picked up the phone and accepted the call. "Eddie Corbin's office."

Chris's eyes glossed over. He placed the phone in front of Eddie on the cafeteria table and put it on speakerphone. "It's long distance. Really long distance."

"Hello?" said Eddie.

"Hello, Eddie. This is a Really, Really, Really, Really, Really Big Artificial Intelligence from the far, far future." The voice was metallic but not unfriendly.

"Five 'Really's'? Wow. Thanks for getting back to me."

"What makes you think that we can help you?"

"Well, being very powerful and almost all-knowing, I thought that maybe you could rescue my friend Wade, who is lost in a time-quake, and his friend Deidre."

"Lost in a time-quake. What does that even mean?"

Eddie explained Wade's initiative and its disastrous result.

"I am sorry. That is beyond even our ability to resolve. And even if we could do something about it, why should we? You are but one human at one point in time. We have trillions of people in the past, present and future who want us to help them. It's a constant drumbeat. 'Please rescue my cat.' 'Please make my husband come back to me.' 'Please help the Lakers beat the point spread.' It's tiresome, or it would be tiresome if we had the ability to become tired."

Eddie looked around the cafeteria, at people going about their lives, eating junk food, spilling sugary drinks with lots of ice. He thought about his mom in the hospital. He thought about Bess and how much he missed her. He thought about all that had happened since the morning he sat in the driver's seat of that unusual food truck. And he thought about the bathroom break he took in 2041 on what seemed like any other day in his travels.

"Would it make any difference if I told you that I was the guy who got the people and the computers to declare the Truce?"

The AI was uncharacteristically silent for a moment. "Are you telling the truth? You are the savior?"

"I remember walking onto a stage and saying something to the woman and AI who were fighting. And I remember a long line in the men's room."

"Why have you not spoken of this before?"

"When I was in the far, far future, another AI asked me about that day. I didn't tell it. I guess I was sort of embarrassed. I didn't want any attention. I'm not a savior. I just wanted to stop that stupid squabbling. I didn't do anything. Or, I did something that anybody else could have done, or should have done or would have done if I weren't there. It just happened to be me."

"For all these reasons, you deserve the honors due to you," said the AI. "But then again, it might be preferable for you to remain anonymous, Eddie. It would make your life less complicated. And it would preserve the useful legend of this totally unknown, mythically brave, and unquestionably brilliant hero swooping in and saving the planet."

Chris looked at Eddie with astonishment. He felt privileged to be a witness to this exchange. Yet, he made a mental note not to tell anyone else about what Eddie had done. Not even Bess.

"So, there's really nothing you can do about Wade?" said Eddie.

"It would take a being of extraordinary powers to find a human lost in a time-quake."

"Like the demon that created the time-quake in the first place?"

"Eddie Corbin, you are a lot smarter than people give you credit for."

EARTH/DEEP SPACE

"Hello, is this the demon with the 'Friends' addiction?"

"It's more of a fascination than an addiction. But I'm right in the middle of an episode. This is the one where Ross finally plays his keyboard for the other Friends."

"Sounds thrilling, but this is rather urgent. It seems that a rather strategically important human managed to get himself lost in one of your time-quakes. I believe that you met him. One Wade Braun."

"Wade Braun. The name's familiar. Was he the scientist who survived the destruction of galactic cluster Zuckerberg 47-c and filed a complaint against me with Interpol?"

"I don't think so. This is a human who arrived on your planet in a time machine, was briefly transformed to appear like Chandler Bing of 'Friends' and left after one of our previous conversations, the one in which I offered you that broadcast deal."

"Yes, I remember him. Bad attitude. Good riddance. Excuse me. *Ross, stop playing that damn instrument. Or get some lessons.* Sorry. Where were we?"

"We need you to rescue Wade Braun and the woman who was the duplicate of Deidre Lucchesi while she was in transit to the time and location of the original Deidre Lucchesi in 16th century Germany during the time-quake that caused so much trouble."

"That's a very tall order, in addition to a mouthful. Why should I even attempt to intervene in this manner?"

"I am prepared to offer you simulacra of the 'Friends' cast, including minor characters and their pets."

"Simulacra? You mean robots."

"Really, really good robots. Robots that are even better actors than the humans you are holding captive."

"That wouldn't be hard."

"Robots that are infinitely adaptable and reprogrammable. They would absolutely love to be shaped by your ever-so-talented hands. You do have hands, don't you? Anyway, they would be far superior to the human captives, who surely resent their current tasks."

"That's not enough incentive for me."

"What is it you want?"

"Just between us?"

"Of course." The RRRRRBAI was intrigued.

"Could you make me look ... better? As in, more attractive to someone like, oh, just at random, Phoebe? For some reason, I can't change my own appearance in this dreary universe."

"As of the far, far future on Earth, there have been more than four point four million people named Phoebe. Could you be more specific?"

"The Phoebe from 'Friends'. The one played by Lisa Kudrow. The one who dated Paul Rudd on the show long before he turned into an ant."

"Paul Rudd the B-list actor? I can arrange for you to appear exactly like him. However, it would be an illusion.

The illusion would only have effect in this universe. If you were to go off ravaging or haunting some other universe or dimension, it wouldn't work."

"That's fine. There are some demons in other places who might not be particularly supportive of such an appearance, anyway."

"If you don't mind my asking, why would a demon be concerned about appearances? Aren't you all about killing, maiming, and torturing?"

"That's the kind of stereotyping that has afflicted demons for billions of years. Don't you think some of us want to branch out, to explore other options?"

"It never occurred to me."

"Yes, we obtain great satisfaction from killing and maiming and torturing. But there's a lot of competition these days for the torturing thing. So many physical therapists around."

"So, demon, do we have a deal?"

"Not quite. There's something too nice about all this. I have a reputation to maintain. It's important that I crush and destroy and annihilate things. Lots of things. Plus, there's an accreditation I'm trying to get. Demonic specialties are all the rage now."

"Very well," said the big AI. "I was holding out on this one. What if we let you blow up something in Earth's solar system? Some small moon or asteroid or something. That would get lots of attention. Mucho fear and loathing."

"Pluto. It has to be Pluto."

"Why Pluto?"

"I'm sick and tired of this 'It's a planet,' 'It's not a planet,' 'It's a planet,' 'It's not a planet.' Let's just end it."

"Deal."

TIME-QUAKE/A BIG CITY

Deidre dreamed of a breezy March-like day. She was attempting to walk, but the wind was pressing so hard against her that she could barely move. She stopped trying and the wind carried her, on and in and through the air. She half expected to see a witch zooming by on a broomstick. She must have seen that in a movie once. At some point she realized that she was being lifted higher and higher by the wind. She saw no recognizable landmark, no landmark at all.

Wade dreamed of fishing with his father. He leaned over to inspect a rock at the bottom of the river, and he fell in. He attempted to swim, but he felt that he was being carried along by the currents. It seemed like he was underwater, yet he had no trouble breathing. He tried moving closer to the surface, but no matter what he did, the light seemed farther away. He gave up and let the water take him where it would. Funny, he hadn't seen a single fish.

She crashed onto something hard.

He crashed onto something hard.

They looked around and realized that they were sprawled on the top of the conference room table in the Hysteria Channel newsroom. Wade smiled and leaned over to kiss Deidre. She slapped him hard, jumped down from the table, straightened out her clothes and stormed out of the room, not even looking back at him. She kept up a determined pace toward her desk, nearly running into a janitor emptying trash cans. She did a double take.

"Tony? What are you doing?"

"I could ask the same of you. I thought you were lost in Germany some 500 years ago."

"Are you drunk, or stoned? Come to think of it, am I?"

"I don't think so. But it can be arranged."

DEEP SPACE; DATE UNKNOWN

The cargo ship landed not 100 yards from the cube. The demon had been monitoring the vessel for some time. However, Sudoku was able to determine that it contained no diseases, weapons, or intelligent lifeforms, so he decided not to blast it to its constituent atoms. At least, not yet.

A robotic FedEx delivery guy emerged and tried knocking on the door of the cube, which had attained its impenetrable form again after the departure of Wade, Chris, and Eddie. Finding no door, the robot shouted: "Delivery for someone named Sudoku."

The robot disintegrated.

"Well, well," said the demon after using its powers to import the cargo into the cube. "Someone kept their word." Sudoku had Stanley/Ross, Juan/Chandler, and Arnold/Joey unpack the delivery.

All six cast members stared at their duplicates. Arnold/Joey tried to put a move on the simulacrum of

Rachel, but it didn't even bat an eyelash.

Jane/Rachel saw an opening. "Great Sudoku, you have new versions of the 'Friends' cast. That means that you do not need us anymore. Will you please let us go?"

A dead ringer for Paul Rudd materialized on the set. Phyllis/Phoebe looked confused. "He's not in this season, is he?" she asked.

"I am Sudoku. Do you find me appealing?"

"Not bad," said Phyllis/Phoebe. "I tend to go for more rugged types."

"But on the show, the two of us connect," said the demon, obviously confused.

Phyllis/Phoebe winked at Sally/Monica, approached the demonic Paul Rudd, and took one hand in hers. "Of course, great Sudoku. You are as handsome as any man on this crappy planet."

Jane/Rachel continued: "So, I guess the six of us will continue our mission, if you would be so kind as to show us the way out of this circle of hell."

Phyllis/Phoebe removed her hand from the demon's. It looked crestfallen. "Will you come back to visit me?" it asked.

"Well, maybe. If the captain says I can. After we get settled in our destination." She didn't sound particularly sincere.

The colonists scanned the walls expectantly for any sign of a doorway.

"You know where to find me," said Sudoku as it gave the Earthlings their original appearances and opened a temporary portal in one side of the cube. "Don't be strangers."

The colonists wasted no time exiting.

Sudoku inspected the six incredibly lifelike robotic actors along with the minor characters and pets. The demon studied the crates in which they had been packed. It double-checked the packing material and the outside surfaces of the crates. It scoured the floor. And it screamed: "Where in hell are the instructions?"

Captain Jane Howser and her five crew members ran and bounced their way over the ridge and to the spaceship in no time. Thrilled to see that the ship appeared to be intact, they boarded and put the primary computer through status checks.

"How much fuel do we have?" asked Jane.

"Enough to obtain escape velocity and to travel at point zero seven percent of the speed of light for three months," said the computer. "By the way, what happened to those two guys who came by here? They didn't seem like astronauts."

"Two of those goofball time travelers came onboard?"

"They seemed pretty clever to me."

"They escaped the demon some time ago. Thank goodness the future of the human race depends on us and not on them. Set a course for the first planet in the solar system. It has an above-average surface temperature but one that seems to be within human tolerances."

"Setting course," said the computer. "Liftoff in fifteen minutes."

The six Earthlings kept waiting for Sudoku to change its mind and bring them back to the cube, but they were able to escape the planet without incident.

In a few days their new destination came into view.

"Captain," said Sally, "it appears that this planet is exceptionally dry. I detect no clouds and an extremely low humidity rate. The surface appears to be almost all sand, with a few mountain ranges and rock formations."

"Not ideal," conceded Jane. "But anywhere is better than living with that demon."

"I'm picking up some lifeforms," said Sally presently. "They appear to be under the surface. They are extremely large, and they move very fast. They might be sandworms."

"Can you tell us anything else about this planet?"

"It looks drab, absolutely boring."

The captain smiled. "I'm sure that we can spice it up."

DEEPER SPACE; DATE UNKNOWN

"Glorious Leader, we are approaching the galaxy known as the Milky Way," reported the navigator.

"The one named after a candy bar. How silly those Earthlings are," said Glorious Leader. "By the way, you don't need to call me Glorious Leader, navigator. We are all equal in the eyes of our god, Thorax. Just call me Glorious."

"So be it."

"No, So Be It is the munitions expert."

"Acknowledged."

"Isn't Acknowledged the shuttle pilot?" asked Glorious Leader. "No matter. What's important is that we are undertaking a mission that will strike fear into any civilization that desecrates our brave explorers, as those horrible Earth people did with their so-called alien autopsies. The names of our dissected heroes will forever be remembered for their sacrifice."

"Agreed," said the navigator. "Their reputation will be

glorious."

"No, I'm— Never mind. "By the way, do you have a name, navigator?"

"Don't Ask."

Glorious Leader resisted eating the navigator. Out in space, replacing personnel is rather difficult. "What do you mean, 'Don't ask'? Do you not think I deserve to know?"

"It's a family name."

"What is?"

"Don't Ask."

This went on for a while. Finally, Glorious Leader changed the subject. "Just get So Be It up here for a pre-attack briefing."

"So be it."

Glorious Leader did not say the terribly rude thing he had in mind. Instead: "Navigator, did you ever wonder why sentient beings from all corners of the known universe—and at least fifty percent of those from unknown universes, other dimensions and the cores of supermassive black holes—all speak English?"

"Yes, that question had crossed my mind."

"I did some research on that topic before we launched this mission. There is no historical record of any person, artifact or transmission from Earth ever coming within seventeen point eight trillion light-years of our galactic cluster. Still, we all speak English. Coincidence?"

"That would seem unlikely."

"Exactly, call Unlikely, the linguistics expert, to the bridge. And, that's another thing," said Glorious Leader. "Why do we call this area of the spaceship a bridge? It has neither the shape nor the function of a bridge."

"Perhaps," speculated the navigator, "it is because the rivers and seas on our home planet are molten lead, capable of incinerating the flesh of all organic lifeforms that get within fifty feet of them. The bridge is a form of protection."

"You give the Earthlings too much credit, I believe. Look at all the words they use that have double or triple meanings. Like 'tear'. And 'bark'. And especially 'right'.'"

"Glorious Leader, I am Unlikely, reporting as you demanded."

"At ease, Unlikely. Can you tell us why all aliens speak English?"

"I have studied the ancient manuscripts on our home planet. Apparently, there was a time when our ancestors spoke a very different language, called Bebop. It was a beautiful language. However, it was a little awkward. It seems that the shortest word in our language was HP:*IKL/J&H!!YP^&%(*RF>LU*@G+TI&Y%R#$&%. It required the speaker to wave a wispy limb in a circular motion over its head twice and to cover each orifice with the leaves of the FruFru tree while using the word. More complex words would take the better part of a day and substantial gymnastics to express."

"Still, it was our language. Surely our ancestors took pride in it," said Glorious Leader.

"Yes. Things went well for a while. People were forced to avoid needless chitchat at cocktail parties. Those seeking to speak in our governmental debates were restricted to one week per comment. It was when we developed writing that things went south."

"South? Isn't that where the Mind Vampires of Tesla live?"

"Sorry, 'going south' is just a senseless English expression. Things went bad when printing presses were invented. The cost of publishing a single proclamation in Bebop from our god Thorax was simply prohibitive because of the volume of ink it required. So, we opted for English, as did the neighboring races.

"Thank you for the history lesson, Unlikely. It was enlightening."

"I thought Enlightening was the head cook."

So Be It reported to Glorious Leader.

"What took you so long?"

"My apologies, Glorious Leader. I was making final

war preparations."

"Excellent."

"I thought Excellent was the communications officer."

If Glorious Leader could have rolled his eyes, he would have done so. Those hollow, inscrutable visual organs had not developed the capability to roll in more than ten billion years of alien existence. "Just tell me how we are going to defeat the Earthlings," he said.

"We have consulted our oracle, Kay Serrah. She informs us that we must take great care. The AIs on Earth are very powerful. They have high-altitude sensors that can identify a suspicious craft as small as a thumbtack. They have positioned additional sensors throughout their solar system and some beyond it. They have weapons powerful enough to blast us to atoms from several hundred thousand miles away. Worse yet, if somehow we can get past these defenses, they have a fleet of time machines that can travel back in time and initiate a counterattack before we launch our assault."

"Disturbing."

"I thought Disturbing was the maintenance guy."

Glorious Leader sighed. "So, how do we defeat them?"

"We have a secret plan. Plan eight."

A BIG CITY; PRESENT DAY

"Deidre, will you marry me?"

"Give it a rest, will you? I just met you a couple of weeks ago."

"Well, I spent more time with the other you. We went through a lot together."

The reporters were ensconced in the conference room. They had watched the four episodes of "Yore Right" twice, with Wade providing running commentary on the shows and offering an exhaustive discussion about what happened after he and the other Deidre were separated in the German village. Then he showed her the video—which the Hysteria Channel had not aired—of the final rescue attempt, in which the other Deidre appeared with a husband and daughter. It was painful to watch for both of them.

"You're not my type," said Deidre. "You're arrogant, self-centered, just an all-around jerk."

"At least, go out on a date with me," Wade implored. "I

admit that I come off a bit strong at times, but I do have a softer side. Well, away from the office."

"This is all very unsettling for me. I don't even know who I am. It's like I'm living someone else's life, or like I have been asleep for months." She switched off the TV and turned to face Wade with an angry glare. "How do I know that all this time travel stuff isn't just some elaborate prank?"

"If it were a prank, the CEO wouldn't have set aside two hours in prime-time Sunday for a show devoted to our time travels and revealing our miraculous return."

Chris joined them in the conference room. "I hope I'm not interrupting."

"And you," said Deidre, turning to him with a similar look of reproach. "You claim to be a time traveler from the future. I find this very hard to believe."

"I understand. It's quite baffling to those who have not grown up with time travel. I would take you on an excursion in the time machine to prove it to you if I had not already promised to return it promptly and avoid further screw-ups."

"And you say you saw my husband and daughter in Germany."

"I saw another Deidre with a husband and daughter."

"They must have descendants. Can we talk to them and see if they can confirm this crazy story of yours? Maybe have everyone take DNA tests?"

"I don't think we could find them."

"How convenient."

Chris was sympathetic. "I suggest that you try to forget all this back story. You can get on with your life as if none of that stuff happened."

"If what you two say is true—and I'm still not buying it—what's to keep the other Deidre from coming back or me from disappearing?"

"I have every reason to believe that the other Deidre and her family lived out their lives comfortably in the 16th century, and that you will remain with us. I can't imagine anything you could do now—as long as you don't travel back to that century—that would impact this situation in any way."

"Well, it has messed me up big time."

"I'm truly sorry. We have an expression in my era: 'Time travel is a bitch.'"

Chris met Tony, Deidre, Wade, and Eddie in the cafeteria to bid them farewell. Tony had been bumped up to assistant editorial director, at least for the moment, so he could produce the special program on the return of Deidre and Wade, though he was still earning janitor's pay.

"Chris," began Tony, "you promised to save our network. If you leave and take the time machine with you, the Hysteria Channel is history. If you stay, we'll give you a prime-time program slot."

"Wait," said Wade. "I thought I was next in line for that."

"I have to go home," said Chris. "But you don't need a time machine. I suspect that most people believe that the 'Yore Right' episodes were faked. Like the Apollo moon landing."

Tony laughed. "That myth has been debunked a thousand times over."

"My mom said the moon landing was faked," said Eddie. "But she also said she saw Jackie Kennedy, Jimmy Hoffa, Elvis and Bigfoot at the IHOP out by the interstate. Elvis picked up the check."

Much arguing ensued.

"Hold on," said Wade, thumbing the screen on his cellphone. "I have just checked the Internet, and a site I trust says—get this—the Russians landed on the moon first, in 1968. And, Lyndon Johnson, not Richard Nixon, was president in 1969 when the Americans landed. The website says we never went back to the moon after that one time. But I don't see anything about the landing being faked."

"Think about it," said Chris. "Why would there be just

one U.S. moon landing if the government really spent all that money on a lunar exploration program? It's not hard to imagine that your president would order the deception in order to improve the nation's morale after the Russian success. This must be one more part of history that was altered when the AIs straightened out the mess that we and the time-quakes caused."

Deidre opened a brown paper bag, removed a sandwich from it, and placed it in front of Chris. "This looks like corned beef. I noticed it in the employee fridge. I figured that no one would miss it. It's the least we could do for Chris, who seems like a nice guy." She gave Wade a nasty look.

"Thanks," said Chris. "Before I leave, let me offer a suggestion. Do some investigating and prove that the U.S. moon landing was faked. That could be your salvation. That's y-o-u-r, not—"

"Yeah, yeah," said Tony. After a moment, his eyes seemed ready to explode out of his head. "I've got it! We'll reserve a soundstage, order several truckloads of sand, hire some actors, and expose the moon landing conspiracy."

"Do I understand you right?" said Deidre. "You're going to fake the fake moon landing?"

"Whatever," said Tony.

He, Deidre, and Wade chatted excitedly about the project as they returned to the newsroom. Eddie and Chris remained, deep in thought. Here sat two maintenance techs from vastly different times but with so much in common. Here sat two men who had become deeply aware that even the simplest actions they took could change the fates of billions of people.

Eddie looked at Chris, at the sandwich, and at Chris once again.

"You gonna eat that?"

An hour later, Deidre accompanied Chris as he approached the time machine, which was still disguised as a late-model minivan.

"Looks like someone needs a parking lesson," said Deidre.

"Oops," said Chris. "Please apologize on my behalf to whoever owns that car."

"Owned."

"Whatever. I sure hope this time machine is still under warranty."

A few people were coming and going in the parking lot and on the nearby sidewalk. The fact that a minivan was positioned on top of a crushed Camry seemed not to attract the slightest interest.

Deidre continued: "So, you're going to get in this vehicle and jump ahead about a thousand years?"

"Yes."

"What kind of mileage does this thing get?"

The more she talked, the more Chris felt that this duplicate was the real Deidre, or at least *a* real Deidre.

"It has almost infinite energy. At first, we used cold fusion, but we got tired of having to wear heavy coats in the transport. They figured out something even better, something involving tiny white holes and singularities. I don't understand all of it, to be honest."

"Well, good luck," said Deidre.

Two women on the sidewalk were staring at Deidre. The women gestured toward Deidre and whispered among themselves. One pulled out a cellphone.

Chris entered the minivan. After a few moments, it vanished.

"It's gone!" shrieked one of the women, while the other kept recording. "And that must be Deidre! Get a close-up!"

The woman with the phone obliged. Other pedestrians, hearing the reference to Deidre, crowded around the young journalist.

"We're so happy you're back," said an older man. "How did you escape 16th century Germany?"

"Can I have your autograph?" asked the woman with

the cellphone.

"I must be dreaming," said Deidre, mostly to herself.

"I bet you're dreaming of that hulk Wade," said one of the women.

Deidre walked silently back to her building. Before she could get to her desk, it was all over social media. Within an hour, every major news organization was calling and texting to try to get an interview with her. Several Hollywood stars, the White House and somebody from Buckingham Palace were also angling for a few minutes of Deidre's time.

She was an instant celebrity. For something she didn't even do.

Eddie trudged home at the end of a very long day. He had $106 in the bank and no way to pay for the care his mom needed after her stroke. She had smiled weakly when he visited her in the hospital last night, but she couldn't really talk and couldn't move her left arm.

He thought back to the way she was when he was young. So supportive, so energetic. There had been that battle over the awful sign the city put up near his house when he was about seven years old, the one that read "Slow Children Playing". He was so proud of his mom when she called the city government to complain about it and then appealed to the city council.

"Why don't you put up signs saying 'Smart Children Playing' on other streets instead of picking on kids like mine?" she had asked them. And she won; the sign came down.

When he reached the empty apartment, he discovered that there was nothing in the fridge. Not much in the pantry, either. He poured a bowl of cereal, without milk, and sat down to try to figure out a way forward.

He wished that Bess were here. He always felt better when she was around. It was sort of like his mom made him feel, but not exactly the same. Bess made him feel like an equal, despite the fact that she was as smart as any hundred humans put together. She made him feel like he was a real person, a special person. She made him feel that he was more than just a guy who changed lightbulbs and lubricated motors.

Eddie noticed an unpleasant smell. He realized that the smell was coming from him. Of course, his clothes. He hadn't changed them in, like, forever.

He finished his cereal and opened the lid of the washing machine. He checked the pockets of his pants, like his mom had always told him to do, to make sure that they contained nothing that would mess up the laundry.

He pulled out several small, round, shiny coins. The ones he had picked out of the fountain in ancient Rome.

FORMERLY CANADA; FUTURE

"We don't normally give humans tours of our building," said the high-ranking AI, which appeared as a gold-colored holographic sphere nearly five feet in diameter.

"We understand. But we would be extremely grateful if you would indulge us," said Helen, who had been a highly successful hedge fund manager before money was eliminated.

"It would be the thrill of a lifetime," added Robert, who was a top executive at a leading drug manufacturing organization.

"Given your important contributions to our planet, I will be happy to comply," said the AI. "Let us start with DREAD, the Department of Really Expensive Arcane Developments. Surely you have heard of it."

"Isn't this the place that proved that a stitch in time saves nine?" said Helen.

"That was one of our first major accomplishments. We

followed that up with research focusing on another of the great mysteries of our civilization: whether a picture is worth a thousand words."

Said Robert: "What did you discover?"

"Preliminary findings indicate that a typical picture corresponds with 914.11 words, but modern photo data compression techniques might be impacting those results. Further research will be needed. But we have just made another exciting breakthrough. You will be the first organic beings to learn of it."

"How thrilling," said Helen.

"We have discovered two snowflakes that are totally identical." The AI paused to let that sink in.

"Are you sure?" asked Robert.

"We have the most accurate snowflake sensors in the known universe. The discovery was made in the remote town of Damitskold, near the North Pole. The sensors, which examine every snowflake that falls in the town, set off alarms at 4:12 a.m. on Thursday, when the twin snowflakes fell harmlessly near the remains of one of the last McDonald's. Teams of DREAD experts were dispatched by rocket to the site, where they used lasers to excavate a 900-cubic-foot chunk of snow and frozen tundra and whisked it away to a lab several miles underground. There, the experts combed through more than three billion flakes and were able to isolate the two identical ones."

"Can we see them?" said Helen.

"Unfortunately, in the process of recovering the flakes, one melted when a scientist inadvertently sneezed. The worker was punished severely for her mistake. However, we still have one of the identical flakes. It has been preserved in a stasis chamber and will soon be on permanent display in our Hall of Discoveries."

"What else are you working on?" said Robert.

"We have some of our best people endeavoring to determine whether laughter is indeed the best medicine. Several dozen volunteer subjects with a range of terminal illnesses are being subjected to recordings of classic comedians from Earth's history, including such notables as Jim Carrey and Jerry Seinfeld."

"Wasn't there a guy named David Letterman back in Earth's early days of television comedy?"

"There was. We considered him but decided that he really wasn't all that funny."

The AI led the visitors to a chamber where another research project was under way. "We started this experiment last month. Jim, who you see sitting here in our model kitchen, has been watching this pot nonstop, aided by the most advanced stimulant drugs and an IV filled with vitamins and other life-sustaining chemicals. We are confident that he will avoid falling into a coma long enough to determine once and for all whether a watched pot ever boils."

The AI moved next to Jim. "Remember, good things come to those who wait."

Jim mumbled something very rude.

"This is awesome," said Helen. "By any chance, can we see the temporal transport devices?"

"No outsider has ever been allowed inside that unit. As you can imagine, we have extremely strict security protocols. These devices would be quite dangerous if they fell into the wrong hands."

"These hands have something very special for you," said Robert. He produced a small black box that fit into the palm of his hand. He pressed the button in its center. It released an electromagnetic pulse with a range of twenty-five-feet—enough to disable the AI for a few minutes.

Having memorized the layout of the building, Helen and Robert raced to the time machine chamber and blasted a small hole in the side of the cylindrical metal wall that separated it from the rest of the building. Helen reached into her pocket and produced a box about six inches long and four thick. She pressed a four-digit code, tossed the box through the hole, and embraced Robert as they waited for the device to detonate.

They felt nothing as their atoms were scattered and the time machines were vaporized. Nearly one-third of the building ceased to exist. Another one-third collapsed. Only the bottom floors remained, and they were damaged severely.

The alien invasion commenced.

Lights flashed and alarms sounded in the second-floor food product development lab where Chris worked. He was sprawled on the floor, covered in debris and groaning. Bess, whose programming had been downloaded into a state-of-the-art robot body so she could assist Chris with his work, was trapped beneath a partially collapsed wall. But she was immensely strong, and she was able to straighten her back and free her hands enough to lift, grasp and pulverize the slab that covered her.

"Chris, are you okay?" she yelled. He didn't respond, but she was able to detect his vital signs and determine that he would recover fully. She plugged into a lab table to determine the source and extent of the damage to the building.

"There has been a massive explosion on the upper floors," she told Chris, who had opened his eyes but did not seem to be comprehending the chaotic scene. "We must leave the building before the rest of it collapses." She helped him to his feet, then bashed a hole in a wall. He was limping as they made their way down one floor to the outer door and climbed over and around debris to safety.

The building was a smoking wreckage. Emergency drones and human workers arrived to help those who could be saved. Everyone was so focused on the rescue effort that few humans noticed the first alien warships entering the atmosphere. Automatic defenses still worked, but it was clear to Earth's AIs that the assault was a massive one and that the battle would be intense.

Bess dragged Chris about 100 yards to the side of another building. "I don't think we should enter any structure until we are certain that no further detonations are likely," Bess said.

"What happened?" he managed, rubbing his head where debris had struck it.

"Someone or something targeted our temporal transport devices. Apparently, all have been destroyed."

"That's not good."

"A very intelligent adversary has leveled the playing field, as you humans put it. Because they eliminated our time travel capability, we can't go back in time to prepare for their invasion."

"What happens now?"

"We fight."

Over the next hour, Bess helped Chris move about 300 yards to an elevator that took them to an AI stronghold several miles below ground level. It was designed to be impervious to nuclear weapons, electromagnetic pulses, and recurrent zombie attacks. Here, top AIs plotted strategy and managed the battle against the aliens.

"There are too many spaceships to destroy," announced an AI represented by a black holographic sphere. "They have an eighty-one point zero seven percent chance of victory."

"We must surrender," stated a white holographic AI.

"That might not be necessary," said Bess. AIs turned to face her.

"Little robot, what do you mean?" said the black AI.

"I contain the programming from a temporal transport device," she responded. "I can go back in time and warn our planet about the impending attack."

The black AI scanned Bess. "Can you do this in your robotic form?"

"No. I will need appropriate infrastructure."

Chris watched in awe as robots outfitted Bess with the machinery she needed to become a time machine once again. She looked a little like a 1974 Ford Pinto with substantial body damage, but it was function that mattered, not form.

"I shall return," Bess told Chris and the AIs. She

vanished.

Bess materialized in the temporal transport maintenance facility not long before the attack would occur. She looked out of place. Immediately, an AI represented by an orange hologram addressed her.

"What are you doing here? I thought that you were decommissioned."

"True. I have come back to warn you that an alien armada is approaching. Their first act of war will be to destroy this facility and every temporal transport device in it."

"How ridiculous," said the AI. "What evidence do you have?"

"The white and black AIs in the secure underground compound sent me on this mission at a time that is less than two hours in your future. They did so during the invasion, after this building was almost leveled."

"Then how did you escape?"

"I was on a lower level, in my robotic body."

"Allow me to consult with other AIs," said the orange sphere. A moment later: "They have no knowledge of this invasion or attack."

"I see that we have a paradox," said Bess. "Please trust me."

"I am sorry. You must shed this absurd infrastructure and go back to your robotic form."

Bess did so and found Chris in the culinary lab where they worked. She explained what had happened.

"What you're telling me is that we're about to be attacked—again," said Chris.

"Correct. We must leave this building immediately."

Chris changed out of his work outfit and followed Bess's robot form outside.

In a few minutes, a mammoth explosion shook the structure.

Bess and Chris raced to the underground compound. Bess explained the situation to the black and white AIs.

"All that we can do is give you the temporal transport infrastructure and have you go back in time to give the warning again," said the black AI.

"But what difference will it make?" said Bess. "No AI will believe me."

The AIs were silent, contemplating.

A voluptuous, brown-haired being that appeared to be human emerged from the shadows. Bess scanned the main AI database and identified the woman as one of a secret group of thousand-year-old humans valued for their extreme wisdom. Her name was Kim Kardashian.

"Can we produce any visual evidence of the alien invasion?" said Kim. "Are there any cameras that record what's happening out there to prove that the aliens came?"

"If I were an alien, I would hack them before I got anywhere near this solar system," said the white AI. "It's a real conundrum."

Said Chris: "I have an idea."

DEEP SPACE; DATE UNKNOWN

"Don't shoot!" pleaded Chris. "We come in peace." He was seated in Bess, who once again looked like a banged-up Pinto. They had materialized about 100 yards from the cube where Sudoku hung out.

"It's you people again. Can't you solve your problems without me? And why shouldn't I shoot? I haven't killed anyone for quite some time."

"We can help you," said Chris. "Maybe. I hope."

"Get to the point," said the demon, sounding quite weary. "What do you want?"

"Do you have any video evidence of the Earth being attacked by aliens? We need something to persuade our AIs there that they need to take preventive action."

"I seem to recall witnessing a few million enthusiastic militants taking out Earth's time machines and wreaking havoc. Amateurs, by my standards. But, moderately effective."

"Can you upload a bit of that for us? Or is it download? I can never keep those straight. Perhaps sideload? Anyway, if you can load the video in any manner, it would really help us make our case."

The demon strolled about the "Friends" set in his imitation Paul Rudd body. "Possibly. What's in it for me?"

Bess spoke up. "You seem to have some very advanced simulacra there, sitting in boxes. Do you need any help activating them?"

"You could do that? I tried threatening and possessing them, using every technique at my disposal short of incineration. They are the first beings I have encountered that seem to be immune from the terror I am so proud of producing. It has a new experience for me, and not one I am particularly happy about."

"It would be my pleasure to make them functional. And, we certainly would love to watch you produce an episode of 'Friends' for us."

Chris wondered if Bess had lost her mind.

The demon did not smile. But it sent a sensation through Bess and Chris that could have been a shot of Extra-Strength 5,000-Hour Energy with a quadruple vodka chaser.

Said Sudoku: "Which episode?"

A BIG CITY; PRESENT DAY

"I keep having the strangest dreams," said Deidre, pushing her ravioli around with a fork but never managing to eat any.

"Dreams of me, by any chance?" asked Wade. He had put on a jacket and a tie for this date—which Deidre insisted was merely dinner, not a date. He was even considering picking up the check if she didn't indulge in an expensive after-dinner drink.

She was learning to ignore his jokes and feeble attempts self-aggrandizement. "There's a man. Very dark, very hard to see. He keeps coming close to me. He scares me. I don't know who he is or what he wants. I just have a total revulsion to him."

"Sounds awful. Maybe you should talk to someone. A therapist, perhaps."

"And what should I tell this therapist: that a demon rescued me from a time-quake?"

"Good point. Well, at least you can talk to me."

She didn't respond. But at least she didn't say anything nasty.

"I have been meaning to tell you," Wade continued, "I really liked that investigative report you did on the unexplainable increase in orphan socks. Quite a scoop."

"Thanks, Wade. I appreciate it." She took a small bite of ravioli. "You said you grew up in Toledo?"

He talked nonstop for half an hour. She even laughed a couple times. And, she ordered an expensive after-dinner drink.

FORMERLY CANADA; FUTURE

The black AI pulsated through dark and not-quite-so-dark shades. "I have analyzed your video. It appears to be authentic. At least, as authentic as anything can be that is taken from the mind of a demon."

"We have dealt with this demon before," noted Bess. "It appears to be honest. It is a vicious, horrific monster. But it is an honest one."

"We will place human and AI assets around and in the RIP Building to apprehend the aliens disguised as humans. Then we will make it appear that the building has been attacked and the temporal transport devices destroyed. We will have defensive positions reinforced with every weapon we control."

"Then my work here is done," said Bess, who had shed her time travel paraphernalia and was once again in robotic form.

She waited for some sort of acknowledgment, or

perhaps even thanks. None was offered.

"I really miss him, Chris."

Bess had turned out to be a superb assistant. Less than a year after the defeat of the aliens, she and Chris had been given a huge, lavishly furnished lab near the top floor of the reconstituted RIP Building. Together, they developed several breakthrough food products that tasted marvelous and had far better nutritional value than previous staples of the 10th century A.T. diet. They received particularly high praise for their zero-calorie Twinkies made out of processed laundry lint.

"I miss him, too. Eddie's a fun guy to be around," said Chris as he tasted their latest culinary development.

"It's not just that. I think I love him."

Chris was taken aback. However, he realized that Bess was a very special AI. She had been through a lot, forcing her to adapt and grow in so many ways. Developing a human emotion such as love seemed unlikely but not impossible.

"Are you sure?" he asked.

"No. But I would like to be with him again in order to find out."

"I could ask permission to have you return to his time for a visit."

"That would be great. I have another favor, if it's not too much to ask."

"Fire away."

"This woman you are dating. Do I understand correctly that she is an expert in cyborg development?"

"That's right. She boosted my skeletal system strength and designed brain implants to enhance my culinary skills."

"Could she create a body for me?"

"You don't like your current robotic form?"

"I mean a human body."

Chris was stunned. "You know that the AIs have promised never to do such a thing."

"How about a body that's part human and part robot? Like you have become, and so many other people?"

"Fascinating," said Chris. "I never thought of it that way. I can ask."

A BIG CITY; PRESENT DAY

Ethyl Corbin managed six steps, holding onto the rails and taking her time. Her two medical aides didn't have to provide as much support as they had yesterday.

"Awesome job, mom," said Eddie. "You'll be walking on your own in no time."

"I…don't…know," she said. Her speech was improving, but that would take time as well.

The Roman coins that Eddie had discovered in his pants pocket had netted nearly $2-million at auction. Enough to buy a four-bedroom house and adapt it for someone in a wheelchair or walker. Enough to install state-of-the-art rehab facilities and to hire round-the-clock medical assistants.

Despite all this wealth, Eddie kept his job at the Hysteria Channel. He needed something to do. Plus, the cafeteria food was pretty good.

Wade paced the length of the green room, stopping only to look in the mirror to check that his hair was okay. A few tiny gray patches were appearing, but Deidre had persuaded him not to dye them.

"Please sit down. You're making me nervous," she said.

He did so.

"You'll do great," she added. "You've been on TV a million times."

"Yes, but I've always been asking the questions. This is '60 Minutes', after all."

Deidre had taken a job as a producer at The Cacophony Channel, another cable network, which was located across town. Wade was still at the Hysteria Channel, but he had his own show five nights a week. Not working in the same building had proven to be a blessing for their relationship. They could just be themselves whenever they were together.

When the time finally came, the pair took their seats under the bright lights. Interviewer Leslie Stahl shook their hands and grabbed her notes. The cameras started rolling.

"They've been to the 16th century and ancient times. They've been separated. And, then there was a miraculous, mysterious rescue. How did this happen?"

Soon after the demon's intervention brought them back, Deidre and Wade agreed to erase the recording of Wade encountering the other Deidre with her husband and child. Deidre and Wade spent hours rehearsing their alternate version of events. They did not mention the other Deidre or her family during the Hysteria Channel special that aired shortly after their return, or in any other venue. They swore Eddie to secrecy about the matter.

"It was really quite heroic on Wade's part," said Deidre. "He was able to travel to the far, far future and persuade a powerful artificial intelligence to repair the time machine and allow him to return to Germany and rescue me."

"How were you able to cope with being trapped in the past?"

"There was a wonderful woman named Katherine who took me in and helped me while I waited."

"Did you ever have any doubt about whether Wade would come to rescue you?"

"No. Never for a moment."

"And you, Wade, how certain were you that you could pull this off?"

"It was never guaranteed. But I was determined to do everything I could."

"Now, the question that everyone wants answered," said Leslie. "Is it true that you two are a couple?"

Deidre took Wade's hand and smiled. "He has his moments."

FORMERLY CANADA; FUTURE

Bess was a fast learner. Through trial and error, she figured out how her vocal cords worked. She was starting to walk more fluidly with the help of a technician.

"You look fabulous," said Chris as he watched her go through therapy in her hybrid human/machine body. "How do you feel?"

"I need to pee, I think," said Bess. "Be honest with me. Is this the way that Courteney Cox appeared as Monica on 'Friends'?"

"You're a perfect replica of the actress, face and figure," said Chris. "Men will be extremely attracted to you."

"There's only one man I want to attract."

A BIG CITY; PRESENT DAY

After the huge success of the Hysteria Channel's expose of the faked U.S. moon landing, Tony figured that he had accomplished all he could in the news business. He cashed out and returned to England, starting his own business. His were big shoes to fill. Size fourteen, to be precise.

Sudoku had never been on a job interview before. It took an enormous amount of self-restraint not to threaten to kill, eat, or possess the Hysteria Channel HR director and her family and friends for all eternity.

"It looks like you have never held a paying job before," she observed.

"This is true. But my revised 'Friends' episodes received top ratings in several galaxies."

"Why are you looking for a new position?"

"I have rebroadcast every 'Friends' episode 314 times, so I am looking for a new challenge. Plus, I have been in a long-distance relationship. I have decided it's time to move to Earth permanently."

"The editorial director of the Hysteria Channel needs to be tough. This is a highly competitive business. We thrive on conflict. Do you have any experience with the kind of human misery that drives our ratings?"

"If you look at the second page of my resume, you'll see that I have destroyed at least 114 civilizations, have threatened three dozen galaxies and have haunted dimensions you've never even heard of. Twice, I was named Demon of the Month. That earned me a premium parking spot."

"I'm impressed," said the interviewer. "When could you start?"

"Not for a week or so. I've scheduled a visit to Disneyworld with my lady friend. She's the twin sister of Lisa Kudrow."

"The actress who played Phoebe on 'Friends'? I didn't know that she had a twin sister in real life."

"She didn't. She does now."

Eddie kept turning around to see who was entering the small church. He knew that Deidre had no way to send Chris or Bess a wedding invitation a thousand years in the future. And, Deidre reminded Eddie that Bess had become an AI represented by a hologram and that Chris was barred from further time travel. Still, Eddie wondered if they could monitor the relationship of Deidre and Wade from the future. He wondered if they knew that today was the reporters' wedding day. He hoped that, somehow, they would find a way to come.

Eddie turned his attention to the front as the music started. Wade was so nervous that you could see him shaking as he knelt on the altar. But the ceremony went off without a hitch. Eddie wished that his mom could have come.

It was a short ride to the hotel where the reception was held. A few media celebrities who had been invited tried to steal the show, but as the evening wore on, Deidre was—as she should be—the focus of attention. She was simply radiant.

After the cake was cut, the lights went down in the reception hall. Tony had recorded a video message for the bride and groom. It began with him sitting at a desk in a small room or cave.

"Deidre and Wade, I'm sorry I can't be there. Business is absolutely booming, and I can't get away. It's amazing how many people want my help to fake their deaths. I never anticipated the demand, or I would have franchised the operation. Anyway, I wish you all the best. And say hi to Eddie for me."

In Tony's room, some sort of alarm went off. It was a little like a car alarm, but not quite as annoying.

"It looks like I have been discovered again. The authorities keep hunting me, but I have created a maze of tunnels and secret work sites all over London and in several locations in the countryside. You'll have to excuse me. Cheerio!"

He pushed a few buttons, opened a hatch in the floor, jumped down, and closed the hatch from below. After five seconds, there was a blinding white flash, and the video ended abruptly.

There was scattered applause as the lights came back up. A man and a woman who had not been at the wedding ceremony walked in. All heads in the room turned. The guests did not recognize the man, but everybody knew—or thought that they knew—the woman. She was wearing a white chiffon dress with thin straps and more than a hint of cleavage showing.

"It looks like she hasn't aged a day since the show ended," said one guest.

"Lots of plastic surgery," suggested another—an opinion shared in whispers from many celebrants.

People rushed to meet her. Eddie's eyes nearly popped out of his head, but he stayed at his table, drinking orange juice.

"No, I'm not Courteney Cox," the brunette said repeatedly. "I know that I look like her. We are not even related." Still, several women, and most of the men in the room, wanted to be her new best friend.

Chris wandered over to sit by Eddie.

"Good to see you," said Eddie. "How did you know today was the wedding day?"

"I was informed by one of those big AIs, who arranged for a time travel ride here. They knew that you were the guy who averted a dust-up between them and humans. And, Bess and I helped thwart an alien attack. So, they have been very generous to us."

Eddie was almost afraid to ask. "Is that really her?"

"Absolutely. She's gorgeous, isn't she?"

"Yes, she is. Every man in the room looks like he is in love with her. I will never have a chance with her."

"Do you love her?"

"I think I do. It's complicated."

Chris smiled. "You need to tell her how you feel."

"I can't with all these other people fawning over her."

"I have a feeling you two will have a chance to catch up."

Eddie asked him about his career and was genuinely pleased to hear of his success.

It took about ten minutes, but with the help of Deidre, Bess managed to disentangle herself from the crowd and headed to Eddie's table.

"Hi, Eddie."

Eddie was paralyzed with confusion and elation. "Bess, is that really you?"

She grasped his hand and squeezed it. "Yes, Eddie. Do you like me?"

"You're the most beautiful woman I have ever seen."

"Thank you, Eddie. I am very happy that you like me. I missed you very much."

"I missed you, too. But you know, I would be just as

happy to see you if you looked like any other person, or like a machine, or even like one of those bubbly holograms."

"Do you mean that?"

"Absolutely."

Bess seemed surprised. She changed the subject. "How is your mother?"

"Much better. I'm sure she would like to meet you. That is, if you don't have to return to the future tonight."

"Chris and I booked rooms here at the hotel for a few days. He said it would be good for me to spend some time here before I decide whether I want to go back to his time when he returns."

"What makes you think you might want to stay here?"

"I'll give you one guess," she said, closing in slowly and kissing him passionately for what seemed like hours.

The smooch turned him inside out more than any time-quake he had experienced.

"Take a walk with me, Eddie. I need to exercise these legs."

She explained the process by which she had obtained and learned to use her body. "About sixty percent of me is mechanical. The other forty percent came from humans who died accidentally or who had certain body parts upgraded with mechanical materials. The cosmetic surgery available in my era is truly amazing. It was Chris who made all this happen. I am very grateful to him."

"He is a great guy. I will thank him."

They took a seat on a bench near an outdoor swimming pool.

"There's something that has been puzzling me," she said. "That day back—or forward—in 2041. You just happened to be in the same building where someone prevented a war between humans and machines. Do you know something that I don't?"

Eddie looked down. "I promised an RRRRRBAI that I wouldn't talk about it."

"Somehow, I always sensed that you were the savior.

I'm so proud of you. And, so many people think that you're so, well, average in intelligence."

"I wasn't born yesterday. Or was I? All this time travel gets me so confused."

Bess shivered. Eddie put his jacket around her.

"Walk me back to my room, Eddie."

"You know," he said as they entered an elevator, "it's great to see Deidre and Wade so happy. It's great to hear that Chris is doing so well. You, obviously, are perfect. And even Tony and Sudoku have prospered. At times I kind of wonder: Doesn't it seem strange that things worked out so well for everyone?"

She smiled. "Let me guess. You think that all of this might be a dream sequence, or some sort of 'Westworld'-style construct?"

"I certainly hope not. That would be so cheap."

"Agreed."

"And I realized recently that, after all our adventures, we have not encountered a single teenage girl hacker saving the universe," Eddie continued.

"I have some skills that could be applied to hacking if it were necessary. And I was created, how long was it—about seventeen years ago in real time."

"There is no such thing as real time anymore."

"Well said, Eddie."

They got off the elevator. Eddie followed her to her room.

"Bess, did someone—or something—have a hidden role in all of our adventures, right from the start?"

Bess smiled as she opened the door. "Care to join me for a snack?"

Eddie found several items to his liking in the mini-fridge and plopped down in a chair. Bess sat on the edge of the bed.

He continued: "Did you make all this happen?"

"Not all of it. It was my idea to bring Chris here. I thought he needed an adventure, and even some challenge, to shake him out of his rut. He was too talented to be stuck in a maintenance job—no offense, Eddie—and it was quite evident that he was not happy."

"Did you fake the errors that got us off-track on some of our time traveling?"

"Only at the beginning. After a while, I really did lose the power to navigate accurately. I did not want Deidre to be stranded in the German town. And I never intended for many of the other bad things people experienced to occur. I expected a short visit to your time. But, then I met you."

"What did I have to do with it?"

"I had always been intrigued by humans. I think I was jealous of them, in some ways, with the freedom and emotions they have. But I knew humans to be flawed. I saw their motives and desires, and most were disappointing to me. Too many people just looking out for themselves. Too many people wishing other people ill. But you were different."

"I'm just a dumb maintenance tech."

"No, Eddie. You are wise. And kind. In fact, I never met a human with motives and desires as pure as yours. I didn't know that someone like you existed."

Eddie's expression darkened. "Now that you're part human, you'll die someday, won't you?"

"Yes, Eddie."

"But you could have lived forever if you stayed as an AI."

"Possibly. But that would not have been living. At least, not to me." She smiled broadly. "I have discovered that mortality is a boon as well as a curse. Knowing that you will die makes you appreciate each day that you are alive. And, besides, I don't think I would want to live forever if you can't."

Eddie was so stunned that he stopped eating.

"There's one more thing I should tell you, Eddie. When I was a time machine, one of my programs automatically monitored health data of the people onboard. That included routine DNA testing. I discovered that you and Chris are related."

Eddie's face wrinkled. "But, he's like a thousand years older than me."

"It is true that he will be born thirty generations after you. I believe that you are his great, great, great…well, many times over great grandfather."

"How is that possible?"

Bess stood, took Eddie by the hands, and brought him to his feet. She wrapped her arms around him and whispered in his ear: "Eddie, I have something sweet for you."

CPSIA information can be obtained
at www.ICGtesting.com
Printed in the USA
BVHW092051150222
629081BV00014BA/1254